Ecstasy Romance®

"PHILIPPE, UNTIL TONIGHT, UNTIL I SAW YOU, I WAS AFRAID TO LET MYSELF THINK OF YOU."

"Afraid?"

Noelle nodded almost shyly. "I was afraid of what you'd be like. Meeting you here tonight was a risk."

"I am different now. But so are you."

She looked down, avoiding his honest gaze. He was right. She'd been a fun-loving girl. But that was before she'd become a woman. Before her life fell apart. "I'm more mature now, Philippe."

"No, Noelle, I don't think it has anything to do with maturity. I see unhappiness in your eyes."

"Please, Philippe . . ." She tried to turn her head. He could see too much, too deeply into her soul.

"Noelle, please don't turn away. We needed each other before but were too stubborn to admit it. Now we have a rare opportunity—another chance. . . ."

CANDLELIGHT ECSTASY ROMANCES®:

186 GEMSTONE, *Bonnie Drake*
187 A TIME TO LOVE, *Jackie Black*
188 WINDSONG, *Jo Calloway*
189 LOVE'S MADNESS, *Sheila Paulos*
190 DESTINY'S TOUCH, *Dorothy Ann Bernard*
191 NO OTHER LOVE, *Alyssa Morgan*
192 THE DEDICATED MAN, *Lass Small*
193 MEMORY AND DESIRE, *Eileen Bryan*
194 A LASTING IMAGE, *Julia Howard*
195 RELUCTANT MERGER, *Alexis Hill Jordan*
196 GUARDIAN ANGEL, *Linda Randall Wisdom*
197 DESIGN FOR DESIRE, *Anna Hudson*
198 DOUBLE PLAY, *Natalie Stone*
199 SENSUOUS PERSUASION, *Eleanor Woods*
200 MIDNIGHT MEMORIES, *Emily Elliott*
201 DARING PROPOSAL, *Tate McKenna*
202 REACH FOR THE STARS, *Sara Jennings*
203 A CHARMING STRATEGY, *Cathie Linz*
204 AFTER THE LOVING, *Samantha Scott*
205 DANCE FOR TWO, *Kit Daley*
206 THE MAN WHO CAME TO STAY, *Margot Prince*
207 BRISTOL'S LAW, *Rose Marie Ferris*
208 PLAY TO WIN, *Shirley Hart*
209 DESIRABLE COMPROMISE, *Suzanne Sherrill*
210 LOVERS' KNOT, *Hayton Monteith*
211 TENDER JOURNEY, *Margaret Dobson*
212 ALL OUR TOMORROWS, *Lori Herter*
213 LOVER IN DISGUISE, *Gwen Fairfax*
214 TENDER DECEPTION, *Heather Graham*
215 MIDNIGHT MAGIC, *Barbara Andrews*
216 WINDS OF HEAVEN, *Karen Whittenburg*
217 ALL OR NOTHING, *Lori Copeland*
218 STORMY SURRENDER, *Jessica Massey*
219 MOMENT TO MOMENT, *Bonnie Drake*
220 A CLASSIC LOVE, *Jo Calloway*
221 A NIGHT IN THE FOREST, *Alysse Rasmussen*
222 SEDUCTIVE ILLUSION, *Joanne Bremer*
223 MORNING'S PROMISE, *Emily Elliott*
224 PASSIONATE PURSUIT, *Eleanor Woods*
225 ONLY FOR LOVE, *Tira Lacy*

THE PERFECT TOUCH

Tate McKenna

A Candlelight Ecstasy Romance®

Published by
Dell Publishing Co., Inc.
1 Dag Hammarskjold Plaza
New York, New York 10017

Dell ® TM 681510, Dell Publishing Co., Inc.
Candlelight Ecstasy Romance®, 1,203,540, is a registered
trademark of Dell Publishing Co., Inc.,
New York, New York.

ISBN: 0-440-16911-9

Printed in the United States of America
First printing—April 1984

*Thanks to Pris and Betsy, who contributed
to the soul of this book.
And to Rose and Kitty who influenced the spirit.*

To Our Readers:

We have been delighted with your enthusiastic response to Candlelight Ecstasy Romances®, and we thank you for the interest you have shown in this exciting series.

In the upcoming months we will continue to present the distinctive sensuous love stories you have come to expect only from Ecstasy. We look forward to bringing you many more books from your favorite authors and also the very finest work from new authors of contemporary romantic fiction.

As always, we are striving to present the unique, absorbing love stories that you enjoy most—books that are more than ordinary romance. Your suggestions and comments are always welcome. Please write to us at the address below.

Sincerely,

The Editors
Candlelight Romances
1 Dag Hammarskjold Plaza
New York, New York 10017

There were a thousand incidents that could have reduced Noelle to a quivering pile of jelly, crying uncontrollably in the principal's office. They all proved she was losing control. *Losing control!* Those were loathsome words to a teacher!

It was the food fight in the cafeteria that finally got to her. Or maybe it was the obscene note at 8:16 A.M. that had humiliated Jerry Blake before his classmates, leaving him in tears. Noelle herself had blanched at the words scrawled by a youthful hand while she consoled the shy Jerry.

Perhaps it was the continued pressure from parents that created the cacophony inside her head. Noelle had talked with the note-writer's father this morning during break. He was shocked, humiliated, and angry. Very angry. He would be in to discuss this incident with the principal later. She had already warned Norm. In fact, this was the third time since 7:45 that she had been in his office.

Admittedly, the confrontation with a fellow teacher just this morning didn't improve the situation. It had been a childish act and never should have happened. Now she would have to apologize. And it was only right that she did. Two adults in the same building with the same goals shouldn't argue over the textbook list for low achievers. They both wanted the same things for the kids. Noelle moaned and buried her face in her hands as the events leading up to that morning's disaster replayed continuously in her head.

By the time the pizza hit Art Garstka's forehead, Noelle had completely lost control of the cafeteria. She tried desperately to prevent the inevitable from happening, to salvage some semblance of order, but within seconds peas were catapulting from forks and macaroni was decorating the cafeteria walls. Few of her normally well-behaved students needed any encouragement to join the impromptu food fight. Indeed, it seemed to Noelle that they welcomed it with an almost malicious glee.

"Home. I think I need to go home," she muttered thickly, between sobs, trying to banish the memory from her mind.

"Yes, that's a good idea, Noelle," Norm Harris agreed, grateful to hear something intelligible from her for the first time in thirty minutes. His rotund belly brushed her arm as he set a cup of water on the desk nearby. "Here. Have some water and calm down. You'll feel better if you go home and get some rest this weekend. I'm confident you'll be feeling fine by Monday."

Norm heaved his perspiring shape into the chair opposite her. What a day this had been! First an irate father met him at the door at 7:30 A.M. to object to unfair disciplinary actions. Then the police drug squad met with him and P.T.A. leaders to present various methods of drug detection in the school, including a dog trained to sniff the students' lockers! A damned dog with a fetish for drugs! The place was turning into a police state!

As if that weren't enough to ruin his day, Noelle and Margaret, two of his best teachers, had a rare run-in over textbooks. All that was before 8 A.M.! Later Noelle warned him about the angry parents who would be in after three. Then the goddamn food fight! It was only 12:30! And now this! Noelle crying in a muddled heap, with no signs of stopping.

"Feeling fine after one weekend? That's what you said before Thanksgiving break. And Christmas. They didn't help," Noelle accused him irrationally, as if all this were his fault. She reached with an unsteady hand for the water.

Norm took a deep breath and eyed her suspiciously. He didn't like the looks of this. "I'm going to ask Myrna to come in and discuss the situation, Noelle."

Noelle raised her glassy eyes as his motives slowly registered. "Myrna?" *The counselor.* Vehemently she shook her head. "I don't want to talk to her

13

right now, Norm. I only want to go home. Home to New Orleans."

Norm glared at her. She couldn't quit in mid-March! Where the hell would he get a replacement at this time of year? "Now, now, Noelle," he soothed her, patting her shoulder. "You can't mean that. You don't want to have to break your contract. Anyway, you just can't admit defeat. It's like climbing back on a horse that's thrown you! You have to go right back into the classroom if you ever want to teach again!"

"I don't want to go back, Norm. Not now. You don't climb back on a horse with a broken arm. Or a broken back!" she snapped, her dark eyes red-rimmed and swimming.

"Noelle, you aren't broken. Just tired. You're too good a teacher—"

Nevertheless, while her class watched a hastily selected film in the audiovisual room, Noelle Clayton gathered her purse, uneaten sack lunch, stack of ungraded papers, and left Grace M. Shackle Junior High.

As she walked through the green-painted door and ornate Doric columns, a feeling of freedom rose within her, like a bird released from a cage. She felt as though she could fly—and wanted to do just that. Fly far away from New Jersey.

At that moment Noelle knew she would not walk back through those pea-green doors of Grace M. Shackle Junior High next Monday morning.

14

CHAPTER ONE

Noelle took one last swipe with the brush, then straightened her shapely legs and spread her toes apart, admiring the shiny color that tipped each one. It was a luxury she had abandoned in lieu of grading papers and preparing lesson plans. It had been quite a while since she had really paid attention to her appearance. But, that was in the past.

She was home now, back where she belonged. *New Orleans.* Back with family and friends who cared. Back to the familiar sights and sounds she loved and had missed so much. Foot-tapping music. Joyous dancing. Rich, chicory coffee. The lazy Mississippi and trees draped with Spanish moss. Oh, yes, this was where she belonged.

Gazing at her Wild Raspberry toes, Noelle thought they looked sexy. She wriggled them again, then arched her feet, appreciating the way her red toes accented each slender ankle. Her calves were firm, with small muscles, slick from a generous slathering of emollient cream. Her hand slid up the smooth length, allowing her robe to fall open. Not bad legs, she conceded to herself, for a woman of thirty-one.

A gentle knock was accompanied by a soft, Southern-accented voice. "Noelle, it's me. Can I come in?"

Noelle tucked the robe around her and tied it at the waist. "Sure, Tina. I'm just doing my nails." She turned a smiling face toward the door even before her sister was through it.

"You look refreshed, Noelle. Did you sleep?" Tina gave Noelle a concerned expression, obviously taking her older-sister responsibilities seriously.

Noelle smiled and stretched like a lazy, Southern cat. "Two hours! I've done nothing but sleep these last three days since I arrived in New Orleans. The trip left me more exhausted than I realized."

Tina nodded knowingly and sat in a chair near the end of the bed. "The last few years have taken their toll on you, Noelle. Face it, you're exhausted. It was a long drive for you to make alone, all the way from New Jersey."

Noelle's dark eyes widened slightly, determined that she wouldn't share her most recent experiences in New Jersey. Sometimes Tina could be so damned mother-henish. "I'm fine now, Tina. You just don't know how good it is to be back home."

"I can't imagine how you managed to stay away

so long. Why, Louisiana has everything and everyone you've always known. It's home!"

Noelle shrugged. "For a few years it was a wonderful adventure to be away. Then, after Mama's death and my divorce . . . oh, I don't know, Tina. Everything seemed to fall apart for me."

Tina's arm encircled Noelle's shoulders lovingly. "Well, don't you worry anymore. You're home now, and Max and I are going to make sure that everything will be fine from now on, starting with tonight. This party is going to be such fun, Noelle!"

Noelle protested weakly. "I wish you hadn't gone to all this trouble, Tina."

"Oh, featherbiscuits! You know how I love parties! And you used to love them too. Actually, I'm glad you gave me an excuse to have this little bash. It's been too long since I've had one. Why, we haven't had the chance to invite all these people at one time since college days. I can hardly wait!" Tina's dark Creole eyes danced with happiness as she sat opposite Noelle.

The resemblance between Noelle and her sister was unmistakable. They shared the same animated expressions and the same large brown eyes. Tina's mouth was more generous, and her smile a bit quicker than Noelle's. Tina's dark hair was coiffed in short, casual curls, while Noelle's ebony waves brushed over her shoulders with each movement of her head. The main difference between them, however, was their height. Noelle's lifelong regret was that she barely topped five foot three, while Tina

17

was a lovely, willowy five seven. Noelle had spent her youth trying to stretch herself into growing just a bit taller, like her older sister. With adulthood, though, she had learned to be content with her short frame.

"Featherbiscuits? Tina, please! Nobody but you would use such an old-fashioned term!" Noelle teased unmercifully.

"When you have a young daughter with big ears —" Tina nodded toward the open doorway just as Brianna, her eleven-year-old daughter, entered the room and plopped on the bed beside Noelle.

"Oh, Aunt Noelle, you're so pretty!" Her face, a striking combination of Tina's dark beauty and Max's angular features, was bright with adoration for her aunt.

"Thank you, Brianna! Come on and join us for some woman talk." Noelle smiled, welcoming the young girl. "You know, of course, you're going to be the prettiest of all," she said sincerely.

Brianna wrinkled her nose. "Not with these braces!" She stretched over to caress Noelle's reclining Persian cat who turned his head sideways to catch every loving stroke.

"Those braces will be gone before you know it!" Noelle promised. "And then, *la petite belle!*"

"Oh, Aunt Noelle, don't—" Brianna blushed brightly from Noelle's compliment.

"You be still, Brianna," Tina chided gently. "Noelle is trying to polish her fingernails. She'll smear every finger if you keep wiggling like that!"

She pushed her chair closer to Noelle's knees. "Here, Noelle. Let me. You never could do your own nails."

Noelle relinquished her brush and bottle of Wild Raspberry, willingly extending her hand for Tina's steady strokes. "I've missed this pampering, Tina. I don't think I've polished my fingernails three times in the last ten years."

"Shame on you! Women need to *feel* pretty in order to be pretty. You should take better care of yourself, Noelle. Come on now. Admit it. Aren't you excited about tonight?"

Noelle shrugged. "Of course I'm eager to see our old college friends. It's just been so long, I'm a little apprehensive. This isn't exactly the best time in my life, you know."

"Let me assure you, Noelle, you're better off than most!"

Noelle rolled her eyes upward. "Heaven help them then! I have no husband, no family, no home, and no job! And you say that's better than most?"

Tina cast her a wistful smile, but didn't answer.

"Look, Aunt Noelle. I brought Mama's old scrapbook. These pictures are so funny! Just look at the dresses! And the cars! There's Miss Sherwin. She's my history teacher now, and oh"—Brianna pointed to a color-faded square photo—"I can't believe she ever looked like that! She was kind of pretty in those days."

Noelle looked over Brianna's shoulder and smiled. "Yes, she was. So, Cathy's still teaching, huh?" A small twinge rankled inside her. If Cathy Sherwin could . . .

"Yep, she's been teaching a hundred years," Brianna commented off-handedly. "And here you are with Mama! Both of you had longer hair then!"

Tina leaned back to admire her work on Noelle's right hand, then nodded with satisfaction. "Those were the days when we had nothing more to do than style our long, beautiful tresses and dress for dates. That was before I had a husband and child and job and a two-story house! Of course, I wouldn't have it any other way, darling!" She tousled her daughter's chestnut curls and started on Noelle's other hand.

"Who's this, Mama?"

"Show Noelle. She knows all these people." Tina hovered over Noelle's hand and concentrated on painting the nails.

Noelle followed Brianna's stubby-nailed finger. "That's Marth-Ann LaBroux."

"Marth-Ann Honeycutt now," chimed Tina.

"Is she still so . . . chubby?" Noelle grinned devilishly.

Amid giggles, Tina explained. "If you thought she was chubby then, you should see her now! She's expecting her sixth child any day! I'm surprised she agreed to come tonight. But if she goes into labor, maybe Bruce Nagle can deliver her. He's a doctor, you know."

"Did he finally make it? How wonderful! He always studied so hard. He even tried to help me pass chemistry one year. Nice guy. I was just too dumb

20

to learn more than H_2O!" They both joined Noelle in laughter, enjoying the show-and-tell.

They chuckled over each photo and Tina related the main points of interesting gossip about each person invited.

"Marge is on her fourth marriage now."

"Timid Marge Habermas?" Noelle asked, amazed.

"She's timid no more! Remember Louise Lushbaum?"

"Who could forget Lush Louise, the one with the big boobs? She was the envy of the entire sophomore class!" More feminine giggles.

Tina arched her brows and lifted her pinky. "She's now Louisa LaRue. Married to a parish commissioner!" Their laughter was tinged with feline relish.

"Oh, Tina, it's so good to laugh again, even if we are being a little venomous!" Noelle admitted, wiping happy tears from the corners of her eyes.

"This is the best one yet!" Tina exclaimed seriously, pointing to yet another photo. "Simone Dunsmore, the one with the airs. Remember her? She married an oil sheikh and moved to Saudi Arabia! Imagine her in a black gown and veil up to her eyes!"

Noelle rolled on the bed, laughing at the mental picture.

"Careful, your nails are still wet!" Tina warned between laughing gasps. "Now, Noelle, I'll admit, I invited a few single men you dated in years past."

"I knew it! I knew it! Don't try to fix me up with a date, Tina. I just don't want any—"

Tina held her hand up to stop her sister's tirade. "Now, listen. You might change your mind. Remember Paul Doherty. Handsome Paul? He owns the local hardware store and handles equipment orders from the major oil companies around here. He's now rolling in money. Only trouble is, he weighs about two-forty, on a strapping five-foot-nine-inch frame!"

"Poor Paul! I can't believe it! He was so handsome!" Noelle lamented with a sigh.

"And Nate LaBraux is single again. He's coming tonight."

"Nate? Is that Nathanial LaBraux? Red hair . . . freckles . . . skinny . . . the one with the low voice?"

"Nate is six-foot-three, two hundred pounds of lean masculinity, and handsome as hell. Works for network television locally and has been married three times. Or is it four?"

"I can't believe it!" Noelle grasped her head in mock distress.

"Who is *this* man, Aunt Noelle?" Brianna pointed and Noelle pushed herself to a sitting position. "He's a real hunk!"

When her eyes found the questioned male, Noelle's heart stopped for a brief, devastating moment. There was something about the intimacy of the photo that brought back floods of memories. Wonderful memories. They were sitting together on the hood of a car, thighs touching, his arm slung casually over her shoulder. Even in an old photo he had the ability to make her heart stop. *After all these years.*

"You remember Philippe Merritt, don't you?" Tina answered quickly.

Noelle swallowed in a vain attempt to moisten her suddenly dry mouth. "Sure," her voice croaked. "Is he . . . married?" What an asinine thing to say! And so obvious! What was wrong with her? So what if he wasn't married? She didn't care anyway.

"I don't know. He was at one time. But I haven't seen him in years, so I don't know what he's up to these days. He's different now, Noelle." She paused and admired her completed work on Noelle's fingernails. "There now, how's that? Not a speck on your fingers, sis. Nice job, if I do say so myself."

Noelle smiled gratefully. "I couldn't have said it better, Tina. Thanks. You know, you'll have to keep this up now. I'll never be able to do them myself."

"It's fine with me, Noelle. It'll give you an excuse to keep coming around after you've found an apartment. I still wish you'd just stay here. You can see that we have plenty of room."

Noelle shook her head. "You and Max have done enough for me already. The least I can do is live on my own."

"Well, I think we'd better finish getting ready for the party, Brianna. And let Noelle do the same." Tina rose to her full height and stretched a little. "Hope you have fun tonight, Noelle."

"I'm sure I will. It's going to be quite interesting, seeing all these people I haven't seen in so long. Like Nathanial, er, Nate, and Cathy and . . . Philippe."

Tina shrugged on her way out of the room. "Oh, I hate to disappoint you, Noelle, but Philippe might not even come. I tried all week, but couldn't get him personally. Had to finally leave the invitation with his secretary, Betty Dunsmore. You remember her. Simone's mother. The one who went to Saudi Arabia with the sheikh. Well, it practically devastated Betty to lose her daughter that way. She's just thrown herself into her work since then. In fact, Betty's such a dear, I invited her to come tonight! Well, see you later."

Tina ushered her daughter out of the room, leaving Noelle with one thought. *Philippe might not even come . . .* It wouldn't have mattered a hill of beans to Noelle, except that she had reacted so strongly to his photo. Like a college co-ed, she had reacted! Memories have a funny way of distorting and enhancing the truth. Oh, damn! Who cares! He's probably married with six kids!

Noelle slipped out of her robe and into bikini panties and a bright green strapless jumpsuit. *Pea green,* she thought with a wry smile as she tied the watermelon-red belt. At least now she could smile about her teaching experiences. And the food fight.

She turned to face the mirror and grabbed a bottle of perfume. As Noelle sprayed behind her ears, across her shoulders, and boldly along her generous cleavage, she acknowledged she had certain assets that Tina did not. Maybe Tina was tall and willowy, but she couldn't fill out a strapless jumpsuit like Noelle! She smiled with pride. Yes, she *was* looking forward to the party! It would be fun!

That night Noelle was aglow amidst her old and admiring friends. They laughed and recalled younger, carefree days and, occasionally took time out to dance to "Cajun Baby" or "Louisiana Saturday Night." It was great to be back!

The small band Max had hired broke into a fiery rendition of "Fox on the Run" and Noelle unconsciously tapped her foot to the beat while listening to Marth-Ann relate hour-by-hour descriptions of birth number three.

"They're playing our song. Care to dance?" A masculine voice rumbled in her ear.

Noelle turned from the circle of attentive females to smile up at her handsome brother-in-law, Max. "It's my favorite tune, and I'd love to!" Max held her lightly and whirled her away over the brick patio. "Thanks for rescuing me."

The lively Cajun music was loud, lifting spirits as well as the leaves of the centuries-old moss-draped oaks. Except for their contemporary dress, they could have been dancing in a bygone era of hoop skirts and elegant Southern mansions. The setting and soft Southern accents were certainly appropriate. Noelle had missed this. Missed it terribly. She threw her head back and laughed at Max's continuous stream of jokes.

He was a good host and brother-in-law. Max knew just when Noelle wanted to dance and that she needed the lightheartedness of a few laughs. It had been years since she had spent any time listening to his jokes. He was a great entertainer. It was no wonder that Max was now chief salesman in charge of the entire state of Louisiana for Lajune Laboratories. He had been with the company for years, and now this mansion of a house was one of his achievements.

Noelle tried not to think about the next day, when she would be apartment-hunting. She hated to leave, but knew she needed to be on her own and away from her family. A week was long enough to live with one's sister, even if they did get along well.

By the time the music ended, Noelle was completely out of breath. "Max, I haven't danced like that in years!" Her cheeks glowed and she gasped slightly as she spoke.

"Hell, nobody in New Jersey knows how to dance to Cajun music, Noelle! I don't know how you stood it up north so long! You, of all people!" He laughed and patted her perspiring back.

"I don't know either, Max. But I certainly did miss all of this. Most of all, though, I missed you and Tina. And Brianna. She's going to be beautiful."

"She is a pretty little thing, isn't she?" he agreed proudly. "But I'm not ready to share her with the irresponsible boys around here! Next year I'm going to encase her in a paper sack until she's twenty-one! Do you think that'll protect my baby?"

Noelle shook her head. "She's not a baby any longer, Max. She's soon going to be a very lovely young lady."

"Don't remind me! I feel so old when she says, 'Did you have rock music in the old days, Daddy?' How about a drink, Noelle? Gin and tonic?"

Noelle smiled and fanned herself futilely with her hand. "Yes! This heat and humidity is getting to me! I'd forgotten how warm it is down here, especially when you dance like we did."

"I'll be right back," he said, walking toward the bar. She could hear him speaking to someone nearby. "Oh, hello, Philippe. Would you like to see our guest of honor? She's right here."

Suddenly Noelle was propelled face to face with Philippe Merritt! She gaped, open-mouthed and pink-cheeked. God! He was still so handsome and broad-shouldered! More muscular than she remembered. Tiny colored dots danced before her eyes momentarily. Was she overheated from the dance? The unaccustomed heat? The stifling humidity? Or was it Philippe's all-encompassing kiss that took her breath and sent tingles of anticipation raging through her limbs?

His strong arms encircled her, pressing her breasts against his unyielding chest. Forceful hands spread across her damp back. She drew in a mouthful of air just before his lips covered hers in a kiss that lasted embarrassingly long. She felt weak and wobbly and couldn't decide what to do with her hands, her body, her loudly pounding heart. Finally her hands found a place on his shoulders, and, of their own accord, inched their way across the sinewy span toward his neck. Her body gravitated naturally against his, grateful to have something so firm to lean on.

Eventually he lifted his face, enough to look into her eyes. "You look radiant, Noelle. Did I bring that color to your cheeks?"

"No, I've been dancing," she sputtered, unable to think straight as she still leaned against him. "I mean, it's g-good to see you, Philippe. What—what a greeting!"

"I was just trying to find out if the feelings that I remembered were still the same. Hope I didn't embarrass you." His eyes penetrated her being, fanning the flames of her desire.

"Of course not," she denied with as coy a smile as she could manage. "What about those feelings now?"

"Much better than I ever remembered." He laughed, then lowered his voice. "You know, Noelle, no matter how hard I tried during the past ten years, I was never able to keep you out of my thoughts."

She wasn't sure how to respond to his rather intimate confession. Her first thought was, *Why didn't you ever let me know?* but she said, "I'm so glad you came, Philippe. Tina wasn't sure if you'd make it."

28

His brown eyes smiled at her. "I'm glad I came too. You're as lovely as ever, Noelle. I wouldn't have missed seeing you for anything."

An old, familiar waltz reached their ears, and Noelle smiled an invitation. "Remember how we danced to that song back in the good old days, Philippe?" Her hands were still on his shoulders, and she started to sway in response to the music.

Philippe covered her soft hands with his and brought them down to waist height. He smiled and squeezed her fingers gently. "Let's have a seat and talk now, Noelle. We have a lot of catching up to do." Philippe moved a step away from their embrace and urged her toward a table with his hand firmly at the small of her back.

"Noelle, Philippe," Max's voice interrupted. "Here, please have a drink. Philippe, is gin and tonic okay?"

"Max, you're the perfect host," Noelle smiled gratefully and reached for the tall, frosty glass.

"And you're the perfect guest," he complimented Noelle graciously, then handed the other tall drink to Philippe. "Still beautiful, isn't she, Philippe. You two get reacquainted and have a good time. I'm going to see if someone else needs a dancing partner . . . or a drink. Excuse me, please."

Philippe looked down at Noelle and she smiled up at him. A thousand questions raced through her mind, yet neither said a word for a full minute. Then Philippe smiled and a warmth spread through her, a heat that seemed to grow in intensity with every additional minute they were together. "Yes. Still very beautiful. Let's take Max's advice and get reacquainted. I want to know all about your last ten years."

"Yes, so do I." She turned and spotted a wrought iron table tucked away near an ancient oak's huge trunk. "How about over there?"

They moved together, and immediately Noelle was aware of Philippe's unusual gait. It wasn't pronounced, but his stride definitely wasn't smooth. It was just enough to be noticeable. Philippe favored his left leg slightly.

She stopped, glancing unavoidably at the ungainly leg. It was then that Noelle really noticed the large size of his upper torso. There was a visible strength in the muscles of his arms and shoulders. His hands certainly had more power than she remembered. Noelle's round dark eyes met his in a questioning gaze. No words were spoken or needed. He knew her, still. Knew what she was thinking.

Philippe smiled tightly, intent on putting her at ease while making light of her curiosity. "It's an old war wound, *ma chérie*. Part of my sordid past."

CHAPTER TWO

"War wound?" she laughed nervously, not knowing whether to believe him or not. "Oh, Philippe, please don't joke about something so serious."

He escorted her to the table, assisted with her chair, then sat opposite Noelle before answering mildly, "Not everyone came back from Vietnam unscathed. I brought my reminder with me. This is just one of a few inconveniences to my social life. It prevents me from dancing like we did in the old days, Noelle. You don't mind if we sit this one out, do you?" He smiled then, and those warm tiger eyes crinkled at the corners. They were wonderful eyes of brown with golden flecks that invited laughter and fun. At least they used to. Were they different now too?

Noelle's emotions were in turmoil. From the intense high of Philippe's kiss they plunged at the realization that he had been injured in Vietnam and still bore the mark. "N-no, I don't mind sitting with you at all, Philippe. I'm delighted to, in fact. It's so good to see you. It's been such a long time since we've been together." She paused, knowing she was repeating herself. It was as if they had rushed to be together, running eagerly, arms outstretched, and now that they were close and almost touching, had nothing to say.

Where should they begin? Noelle wanted to know so much about him. There were a million questions to ask—and answer. Right now it was sufficient just to look at him, to assess the angular lines of his face, to wonder about those deep furrows in his forehead, the tiny scar under his left eye.

Philippe's hands lay casually on the table, framing the tall gin and tonic. They were tanned and long-fingered and reminded Noelle of times when he had held her, caressed her face, clutched her own small hands. There was a strength evident in those hands, even as they lay relaxed. Her eyes traveled up the navy sport-coat sleeves to where broad shoulders jutted, almost too broadly for his height. His shirt was white and open-necked, revealing a faint smattering of golden chest hair. She could see the sinewy cords in his neck as he leaned forward on his elbows. The power, the strength that radiated from him now, as they sat, was awesome. She could see it, almost feel it. Suddenly Noelle wanted to experience his arms around her again, to know that strength. His firm mouth moved and all she could think of was that kiss. *That kiss!*

"Noelle, why did you come back home? Are you here to stay?" The band paused between songs and silence hung heavy between Noelle and Philippe, as if these casual-sounding questions were the most important ones in the world. Something in Philippe needed to know. Something in Noelle wanted him to care.

Strains of the old rhythm and blues tune, "St. Louis Woman," filled the background, and a smile reflected her pleasure at the sounds and sights of the evening. It was simply another reminder that she was back home.

Noelle reached out spontaneously, and caressed his left hand. Her finger traced the trails of upraised veins. "To answer your second question first, yes, I'm here to stay. That is, if I can find a job and an apartment. The reasons why I came back are more complicated, but basically, I missed this place and these people like crazy." She smiled and brilliant teeth flashed against her darkness.

"All I can say is, I'm glad you're here. Now that I see you, I wish I had tried to get in touch with you sooner, Noelle. I wish . . . oh, God, it's good to see you!" His right hand covered hers, holding it tightly. She could feel the warmth radiating through this physical link between them.

Her fingers moved ever so slightly, caressingly, between those two masculine hands. "You aren't married?" She licked her lips nervously, hoping he would say no, feeling deep down that he wouldn't have greeted her with that kiss if he were married.

33

"No. And you?"

She shook her head. "Not anymore. I've been divorced for two years. Tell me all about yourself, Philippe. Have you always lived here in New Orleans? Where do you work? The rice farm?"

He took a deep breath and moved his hands from hers, taking a long drink of the gin and tonic. She could almost see the tension drain from him, watch him begin to enjoy the evening. The strain of their meeting had affected both of them, apparently.

"I run a commodities export company here in New Orleans. It started with rice, chiefly from my own farm. We've branched out to include cotton, timber, iron, and steel shipped down the river and across the world. Nowadays petroleum is big." He shrugged as if it were a simple farming operation. But Noelle knew that petroleum, as well as iron and steel shipping on the Mississippi, was big business.

Noelle fingered her glass. "Well, sounds like you have quite an operation going there. I'm impressed. When I knew you before, the rice farm was the major business. You and your father were struggling over expansion."

"That's putting it mildly," he chuckled. "My father and I argued constantly over expansion and direction of the company. After I returned from Nam, it was inevitable and necessary. The work kept me busy at a time when I needed it."

"Do you still have the plantation? It was so beautiful." Her memories were vivid of Sunday afternoons spent with Philippe's family, swinging on the porch, walking hand-in-hand by the creek, kissing beneath swaying trails of Spanish moss.

"Yes, the house still belongs to the family; however, I'm afraid it's not the same as you remember it. But, then, none of us are the same, are we?"

"Somehow I feel as though I should be calling you 'Mr. Merritt' after all that. You've changed, Philippe."

He laughed and shook his head. "Don't embarrass me, Noelle. We'll always be close. I'd like to think we could pick up where we left off ten years ago. Those were good times we had together. I've missed them. But most of all, I've missed you. I've thought of you often in these past years." The tone of his voice told her he was serious, and she believed him.

"Have you, Philippe?" She held her breath, thinking of the times she had been alone and lonely, wondering if he had too.

Where had he been in those years that he could have had the freedom to think of her? Had there been no other women in his life? No special woman? Realistically, she knew that couldn't be. He was too virile, too handsome, too wonderfully masculine to remain alone. The thoughts of him with other women filled her with agony. She knew, at that moment, that she wanted him, desired him with a feminine longing she had never felt for any other man.

His words were mild compared to what she was thinking. "Of course. It's only natural. You were—

are a special memory, Noelle. The times we shared in college were fun and carefree and . . ."

"Innocent," she filled in with a smile.

"Yes, innocent. Didn't you ever think of me, Noelle? Didn't you ever wonder . . . ?"

"Yes, of course I did, Philippe. But, I, well, I was married for three years." She shrugged. "Two of those years kept me busy trying to make the marriage work. But the love just wasn't strong enough, if there was ever any love at all. Now, sometimes, I wonder." Her dark eyes lifted to his, and suddenly a mutual understanding created a strong bond between them. This magical attraction had lasted for ten years. Was that strong enough? Certainly it was strong enough to pursue.

He looked down, his voice low. "I understand. I was married before too. But that, too, is over."

"Philippe, until tonight, until I saw you, I was afraid to let myself think of you."

"Afraid?"

She nodded almost shyly. "I was afraid of what you would be like. Your memory was too perfect to spoil. Meeting you tonight was a risk. What if my dreams of you had been destroyed? I didn't want to take the chance."

He shifted. "Noelle, I am different now, but so are you. I can see it in your eyes. They've lost some of their sparkle. They were full of laughter and happiness. Do I detect a little sadness now?"

She looked down, avoiding his penetrating gaze. He was right. She had been a free-spirited, fun-loving girl. But that was before her life fell apart. "I'm just more mature now, Philippe."

His finger lifted her chin, caressing it softly. "No, Noelle, I don't think it has anything to do with maturity. I see unhappiness in your eyes."

"Please, Philippe—" She tried to turn her head. He could see too much, too deeply into her soul.

"Noelle, please don't turn away from me again. We needed each other before, but were too stubborn to admit it. Now we have another chance. Not everyone gets that opportunity." He moved his hand, but his searing touch remained.

She smiled gently, knowing he spoke the truth. "I must admit, it made me angry when you joined the navy. I was furious that you would go away from me, risk everything in Viet Nam just when things were going so perfectly between us. And they were good, you know."

"Didn't you understand that I had no choice? My older brother was already in the service. It was my turn. The pressures from my father were tremendous. And when Dominic was killed, those pressures became impossible."

"I'm sorry about your brother," she offered quietly.

"Me too," Philippe admitted honestly. "Such a damned great loss! He was the only one in the family I could work with and I still miss him." He lifted sober, brown eyes, then smiled. "Actually I was miffed that you would move so far away, to god-

37

damn New Jersey! I just couldn't believe it! Not my little Cajun baby."

They laughed at his wonderful old nickname for her. It was a teasing, yet loving endearment.

"You couldn't imagine the torment I endured up there. My Southern accent, my expressions, my temperament . . ."

"Do you mean that they didn't like your sassy ways? And that's what I loved so about you!"

Loved? Noelle closed her eyes and caught her breath for a moment. "No, Philippe. It was. . . . so very different there. And difficult for me."

"I can tell it was. I'm glad you're back. Very glad. Now you can be yourself again, Noelle."

She looked at him wistfully. Would she ever be herself again? "I hope so, Philippe."

"Of course you can! When you get a little shrimp gumbo and chicory coffee and Dixieland jazz in your bloodstream again, you'll be the same as always!"

She laughed, delighted with his words. "You remembered my love of New Orleans–style jazz."

"Oh, yes, I remember, Noelle," he reflected softly. "Old Preservation Hall hasn't been the same since you left!"

"And you still like the progressive sounds?" She wrinkled her nose.

"But, of course! Mr. B, Shelley Manne, the Duke, and Dizzy are still my favorites."

"I'll bet you haven't been entertained by the *real*

jazz of Satch or Errol Garner or even our own local Pete Fountain since I left!" she chided.

He smiled. "No. Nor have I had a good argument about what is real jazz. Progressive or traditional. It's about time to revive our old pastime too!"

"Great! I love a challenge!"

"You always did, Noelle. You're sounding more and more like you used to. Now, tell me, what kind of job are you looking for?"

Her answer was readily eager. "I'm a teacher. I have degrees in art and history and taught both in New Jersey. I'm planning to do the same here. Of course, art is my real love. Tina says there's an opening for an art teacher at the private school where she teaches. I'm going in Monday to fill out an application."

"A teacher, huh? I'll bet you're a good one, with all that energy and the way you love kids."

"I like to think I'm a good teacher," she admitted. "I love it. It's just about the perfect job. The hours are great, plenty of time off for vacations, and touching kids' lives gives you such a wonderful feeling of accomplishment. I'm anxious to get started here."

"I'm expecting the violins any minute," he said with a teasing grin. "Noelle, if you love it so, why did you quit teaching in mid-semester? Didn't you have to break your contract?"

She took a drink and smiled a false smile. "Things weren't going very well for me in New Jersey. I just felt it was time to move on," she shrugged as if teachers moved on in mid-semester all the time.

"I see," Philippe said, deciding now was not the time to pursue this. "Well, I'd like to see things go well for you here in New Orleans. Can I help you in any way? Maybe I could give you a hand finding an apartment."

"Well, I'd planned to go tomorrow afternoon and look at some rentals advertised in the paper. Tina and I—"

He interrupted persuasively. "Let me take you. I have a couple of very nice places in mind."

"Okay," she smiled, and suddenly the idea seemed a very pleasant one. "I'd like that, Philippe. Very much."

"It's a deal then. I'll pick you up at ten." He concluded.

During the course of the party Noelle danced with other men, laughed with other friends. However, Philippe's arms were the only ones she cared to be in. He was the only one who lingered in her mind long after the music died down. Noelle found herself looking forward to ten o'clock Sunday morning.

Dancing with tall, handsome Nate LaBraux was an experience in endurance. By the time the music ended, Noelle's fingertips tingled from stretching her arms straight up to reach his shoulders. Why, they couldn't even talk when they danced. Her mouth lined up with his chest and her nose could easily fit under his armpit. It was not the most comfortable position for dancing, and she couldn't wait for the slow song to end.

Nate didn't seem to mind that he couldn't whisper in her ear. He probably was accustomed to towering over everyone, especially women. She felt overwhelmed by his height, intimidated by his hugeness. Nate promised to see her later, and Noelle wondered what she would tell him. *You're too tall. I feel like a child next to you. Find someone your own size, Nate. And I have no desire to get in line behind the many women in your life!* Of course, she wouldn't say any of those things to him. She was too polite. But Noelle knew that being in Nate's arms was like . . . nothing.

Now, Philippe was another matter altogether. His five foot ten frame wasn't too tall. Nor too intimidating. Their bodies fit just right. At least, if he had held her in his arms to dance, she was sure they would have matched. But Noelle and Philippe didn't dance together all evening. Philippe didn't dance with anyone. He was different now. He had admitted it. He was . . . crippled.

She thought about him, late that night, wondering what kind of hell he had been through in the war. And afterward, with his injuries. Obviously the wounds had been serious. Had there been a devoted woman who loved and supported him? Was he married then? Or was he alone? She shrugged away the latter thought. Knowing Philippe, he was alone only when he wanted to be.

Noelle glanced at the clock. Three A.M. Her insomnia usually didn't keep her up quite this late, but this had been an exciting evening. She rose and walked to the window. A silvery half-moon hung just above the top branches of the huge magnolia tree outside her window, casting a faint glow to the world below. It was a world she loved, and she was grateful to be back home in her beloved New Orleans. Now maybe everything would be all right. She curled back in bed and hugged the pillow, squeezing her eyes shut, willing the night away.

At ten sharp the next day, Philippe stood at the door, looking exceedingly masculine in gray slacks and navy and white linen-knit sweater. His waist and hips were trim, but the massive muscles in his biceps and shoulders unavoidably drew Noelle's gaze. The shirt's weave lay intimately, enviably, against his bronze skin.

Noelle caught her breath, taking him in from his casually combed chestnut hair to his calfskin loafers. It was all she could do to keep from throwing her arms around his neck. She had a wild desire to see if their bodies really did fit together as well as she had imagined during the early morning hours. But Noelle Dupree Clayton only smiled nicely at Philippe Merritt and slid her hand modestly into his.

"Ready? My God, you're beautiful." His tiger eyes glinted with pride, and he led her to his steel-gray Mercedes.

"Thank you," she murmured, smoothing the skirt of her turquoise sundress as she sat beside him on the plush burgundy seat. "It's going to be a great day, Philippe. I really appreciate you taking me around. Looking for apartments can be so boring."

"Nothing's boring with you and me!" he promised as he started the engine with a roar and whisked her away. Before long, they were threading through the narrow streets of the *Vieux Carré,* the French quarter. They drove down familiar Chartres Street, past picturesque Jackson Square, to crowded North Peters Street and the always-open Café du Monde in the French market. "How about our old favorite café au lait and beignets?" He looked triumphant, knowing she would love it.

Noelle smiled with eager anticipation. "Great! Sounds fantastic! Just like old times."

And, just like in old times, they were serenaded by impromptu jazz combos gathered in the grass and on the street corners. Music and spirits were high and, as Noelle listened to every long-missed note, Philippe razzed her good-naturedly about the discordant sounds. It was great fun, and they laughed together, loving the roguish exchange again. By the time the coffee and doughnuts were gone, they were clasping hands, leaning shoulder-to-shoulder, touching because they couldn't help it.

Philippe drove her around the French quarter again, down the scenic view along the Mississippi River, to the elegant frontage around Lake Pontchartrain. The apartments and town houses they inspected were exquisite and lovely. Noelle oohed and aahed in every room, but found something amiss with each one. Finally, with a rueful expression, she halted Philippe.

"I don't know how to tell you this, Philippe, but while these places you've shown me are beautiful, they're just not right for me. You see, on a teacher's pay, I simply can't afford them."

"Oh, Noelle, why didn't you say something sooner? My condo is near here and I just assumed—well—I assumed too much. Actually I should have known. You shouldn't have to tell me." Quickly he escorted her back to the car.

He drove through a lovely older part of the city. "What kind of place would you like, Noelle?"

"Well, I know it's probably too much to ask, but I'd love a patio. I had a tiny, ugly place in New Jersey, with no yard. Now I have a yearning for a tree. A Louisiana tree draped with moss. The apartment doesn't have to be big. I just need enough room for me and Louie."

"Louie?" Philippe frowned at the mention of a masculine name. "The man in your life?"

"Um-hum," Noelle nodded smugly. "He's the only male in my life. My cat, Louie."

"Ah, after Louis the Fourteenth? That's a good name for a New Orleans cat."

"No! After Louis Armstrong!" she laughed. "Although he's like most Frenchmen. Very independent, stubborn, and prefers his *liberté!*"

"Does he like your jazz?"

"Of course," she smirked.

"An apartment for Louie, the cool, jazz-loving

44

cat!" Philippe laughed. "Well, that should be easy enough. Let me see now. How about St. Charles Street?"

"Nice area. It has the trees I love," Noelle nodded.

They followed a green and gray trolley car down the tree-lined boulevard until they came to the driveway of a huge old estate. A beautiful remnant of another time, it was now surrounded by houses, apartments, and highways. An antique cornstalk wrought-iron fence squared the small yard while hearts wove intricately across the front balcony railing. By mentally blocking out the rush of traffic on the street and the closeness of neighbors on all sides, Noelle could imagine the house in another era. A step back in time. She loved it immediately.

"Oh, Philippe, how beautiful," Noelle breathed.

"Do you think it might fit your requirements for an apartment? The best I can remember, there is a huge live oak in the back. Don't know about the moss."

"It's for rent? This place?" Noelle gaped, open-mouthed, then shook her head. "I told you, Philippe, I can't afford . . ."

"Not the whole house, *ma chérie*. Sometimes Aunt Donda rents an apartment or two when she knows the reputation of the prospective client. Let's go in and meet her." His hand clasped Noelle's, weaving their fingers intricately and giving her an affectionate squeeze.

"Your aunt?"

"No, not really. That's just an endearment. We became friends when I worked with her husband a few years before his death. Since then, I've tried to keep an eye on her. If she has room for you here, I'd love to keep an eye on both of you. Come on."

The elderly lady who greeted them fit in perfectly with the elegant, grand image of the house. She was, indeed, a woman of another, more formal era. Her slender form was clad in a mauve and lace dress reaching almost to her ankles, and her gray hair was piled into an elegant knot. Her hand rested gracefully on a cane, as if it were an ornament of style instead of an instrument of necessity. She was obviously very proud. Her alert but faded blue eyes lit up when she recognized Philippe, but raked over Noelle as if to determine her worth. When Philippe said Noelle was a schoolteacher, that was the only character reference Aunt Donda seemed to need. Her aged smile said it all.

"Here's the key to the attic apartment, Philippe. You take her up and show her around, please. You have to use those outside stairs. I can't climb them anymore." Aunt Donda shrugged them away with a wavering, paper-skinned hand.

Philippe led Noelle through the musty, antique-filled house and onto the back patio. A huge, century-old live oak draped with gray-green Spanish moss shaded the entire yard. To the side, a magnificent shiny-leafed magnolia lifted branches above the roof of the two-story house.

"Philippe! It's perfect! How gorgeous!" Noelle exclaimed.

"How do you know it's perfect? You haven't even seen the apartment, yet."

"I've seen enough! This patio is perfect! I love it!" Full of excitement, Noelle followed Philippe dutifully up the outside stairs that led to the apartment. It was just large enough to be adequate. The ceilings were slanted and dormer windows admitted plenty of light. "Yes, it's perfect! I like it, Philippe. Living room and kitchen in here and," she muttered, half to herself as she wandered into the sizable adjoining room, "and the bedroom in here."

Philippe stood close behind her. "With a little paint this place could be okay. Can you imagine sleeping in here, so close to the upper branches of that oak? And the fragrance of the night-blooming jasmine coming in through raised windows? I can . . ." His voice dwindled into a low sexy sound. "Noelle . . . come here . . ."

She turned to him, and their bodies melded immediately, as if their thoughts were of one accord. It was a natural blending. And wonderful. Noelle was in his arms, touching him, clinging to his strong shoulders as she had longed to do the minute she saw him. He released within her a feeling of abandon, a freedom to love, to desire. With feminine longing she pressed her breasts against his unyielding chest.

Philippe's kiss was tender and loving, but growing in intensity with each breathless moment. His tongue tasted the edges of her lips, then dipped inside to savor the sweetness of her mouth. Noelle responded, opening wider to admit him, touching his tongue with the tip of hers.

Her message was obvious and only increased his yearning. A low groan swelled within him as his arms enfolded her, molding her soft curves to his hard muscles. One hand moved ardently down to the small arch of her back, pinning her hips to his.

Theirs was a heart-stopping, longed-for blending of man and woman, fitting together perfectly. Wonderfully. Neither wanted to break apart, but each knew this magic moment couldn't last. This was neither the time nor the place.

Philippe finally lifted his head, his voice thick with emotion. "God, Noelle, I want you. I want to make love to you. I've thought about you for years. Now that you're here, I can't wait for you any longer."

"I know," she murmured and kissed his lips softly. "I want you, too, Philippe. Here . . . but not now. I'm just not ready yet."

"I don't want to wait. I want you now!"

"Philippe, I want it to be special . . . perfect for us. Please, give me time. I'll be moved by next weekend. It'll be perfect, I promise! You've waited ten years. Surely you can wait another week." She smiled faintly, knowing it was a lot to ask of him.

"Noelle, I don't want to wait."

"Philippe, it's . . . it's happened so fast, I—I need a little time. Please, try to understand." She needed time to understand this for herself. Couldn't he see that?

He sighed the next word. "Understand? I know only that I want you. And you want me, too, Noelle. You know it."

"It's more than just wanting, Philippe. I wish it were that simple. But there's more between us than that. Things are happening, changing so fast. I need a little time. Don't rush me. Please."

A frown deepened the furrows in his forehead and the faint scar under his eye seemed to stand out. "Next weekend?" He sighed and moved away from her with effort. He turned to stare unseeingly out the window. "I won't be here next weekend. I—I have to be out of town."

Noelle slipped her arms around his chest from behind and rested her cheek against his back. "Do you have to go, Philippe?" She wanted him, too, with a strong, aching desire. Maybe they shouldn't wait.

"Yes. I have to go." The answer was hard, but his next statement sent a cold chill through her. "You're right about complications in our lives. I didn't tell you earlier, Noelle, but I have a child in Houston."

CHAPTER THREE

His voice was tight and distant. "I have a daughter, and I hardly know her."

"A . . . a daughter?" Noelle was stunned. She knew Philippe had been married. But in all the time they'd spent together, he hadn't mentioned the wife, much less a daughter. Somehow Noelle imagined Philippe alone and lonely for ten years without her. Now she knew that was folly. He had loved . . . and had been loved. The knowledge hurt.

He turned back to her, the lines on his face taut. "My little Rose is eight years old and lives in Houston with her mother. I seldom see her. When I do, the meeting is strained. It's like we are strangers. I suppose we are." There was a sad, hollow admission to his tone.

"Give yourself time, Philippe. She's only eight."

He shook his head, those tiger eyes severe. "I'm afraid I'll lose her completely if I don't work at this now. That's why I have to go to Houston next week. I'm trying to coordinate most of my business there, so I can spend some time with my daughter. I really want . . . need to see her. Now, though, I want to be with you, too, Noelle. This is the first time I've ever had a conflict of interests. Rose has always been first in my life." There was a glimmer of a smile in his intense eyes.

Noelle took both of his hands in hers. They were no longer warm, but icy with emotion. "I'm flattered, Philippe. But I understand. Of course you should be with your daughter every chance you have. I can tell it's very important to you. And . . ." She shrugged. "I'll be here when you return."

"Rose has always been the most important person in my life. But now, suddenly, you're back, Noelle, and I don't want to lose you again." He lifted her hands to his lips and caressed the knuckles, letting his heated kisses trail down each finger.

Noelle's breath came in gasps at his very tender, but sensuous act. "You won't lose me, Philippe."

"Promise?" He pulled her close again and kissed her smiling lips.

"Of course," she agreed. "I'll be busy this week anyway. I'm going to apply for that job tomorrow. Then Tina knows where I can find some very good second-hand furniture. By the end of the week I'll be moving in and getting settled."

"I wish I could help you with all that. Tell you what. When you're ready to move, call my secretary, Betty. I'll leave a message for her to get a couple of the men who work in the warehouse to move you."

"Philippe, you don't have to do that. I can manage."

"I know I don't have to. But I want to help, Noelle. I want you here and settled when I return." His lips brushed hers softly as he whispered, "I want you very much. . . ."

"Philippe . . ." The word was a plea of desire that pulsed through her limbs, and she leaned magnetically against his hard, virile body. She had never felt so drawn to anyone, so secure, so unassailable. She had an irrepressible urge to pull him into her very soul. To absorb his strength into her weakness.

In one slow, deliberate movement, his lips covered hers, his arms enfolded her, his entire body molded to surround her, to engulf her. Noelle felt invulnerable when he held her like this. She absorbed his strength whenever he touched her and was alive with passion. Waiting the week for Philippe's return would be as painful for her as for him.

The power of Philippe's masculinity was overwhelming as he crushed Noelle to his unyielding body. He was stronger than she ever remembered, and she seemed to soar in his arms, forgetting the injury to his leg. Weakness wasn't a part of Philippe's personality, nor of his physical being. Certainly there was nothing weak in his grip. His seductive power whisked her away to a sweet, sensuous cloud of perfection.

His lips claimed hers, fiercely this time. The

strength of his masculine arousal was obvious as she was forced against his thighs. For a glorious moment Noelle forgot the problems that had made her abandon her home and job in New Jersey. She forgot the drudgery of moving that lay ahead of her. She forgot the differences that tugged at her and Philippe. She could think of nothing but the desire she felt for him and the infinite pleasure of being held in his arms.

"That teaching position has been filled, Tina. But Sister Agnes will keep my resume and application on file," Noelle explained morosely. "Now what? There aren't a lot of openings for art teachers, you know."

Tina served tall glasses of iced tea to both Noelle and Max before seating herself across from them. "Don't worry, Noelle. We'll find something for you. I'm sure, in a city this size, there's a job just right for you."

Noelle shook her head. "I'm not so sure, Tina. And I really can't afford to live very long without a salary. Oh, maybe a couple of months. It'll be three months or more before they process my resignation from the New Jersey public schools, and I receive my retirement money. Meantime, I struggle."

Max leaned forward and rested his elbows on his knees. "Now, Noelle, you know you can depend on us to help you in every way, including financially. We'd be happy to loan you money, if that's what you need. In fact, you don't even have to move into that apartment this week. Wait a while before making that move."

"He's right, Noelle. We'll help you in any way we can," Tina agreed.

"Already you both have been more generous than I deserve. I really appreciate all your help so far, but can't impose any longer. I need to get established on my own. I might have to take you up on a loan if things don't come through for me."

Tina smiled enthusiastically. "We'll start a blitz on the want ads and schools in this city like you've never seen, Noelle. Something will turn up. You'll see."

Noelle smiled, cheered somewhat by her family's encouragement. "I love your positive attitude, Tina. And your ideas for the old brown wicker furniture we found are super. As soon as I move in and get settled, I'm going to spray it all white. It'll look great. I just can't wait to see everything in the apartment."

"Do you really like that furniture? Honestly, Noelle? Actually, I would have chosen something a little more . . . elegant," Tina offered.

"You're talking expensive," Noelle laughed. "No, thank you. This sturdy wicker will do just fine. A person without a job can't afford to be elegant!"

"Don't be silly, Noelle. You'll have a job within two weeks! Why, when they see your credentials, they'll flock to your doorstep!" Tina promised spiritedly.

Friday Noelle began moving into her quaint little

apartment with the generous, moss-draped trees and beautiful patio. Assistance came from Philippe's warehouse employees, Max, Tina, and even tall, handsome Nate LaBraux. Nate had been very friendly since the party, and now, during the move, extremely helpful. For someone who had been so unmuscular and downright clumsy in his youth, he was now surprisingly strong. He was exceedingly handsome; not to mention *tall!*

Noelle had to admit that Nate was no slouch when it came to lifting the heaviest items. He even helped the movers negotiate the refrigerator up the treacherous stairs. It was Nate's suggestion to arrange the sofa and chairs before the floor-to-ceiling window, thereby providing a lovely, over-the-tree-tops view while giving the visual feeling of two separate rooms between the kitchen and living room. He stayed the entire day, contributing unfailingly until it was time to get ready for his appearance on the nightly news. Oh, yes, Nate LaBraux had been such a tremendous asset on moving day that Noelle couldn't discourage him.

The weekend was so actively filled with cleaning, arranging and rearranging furniture, and unpacking, that Noelle barely had time to miss Philippe. Barely. She dreamed of him at night, recalling her promise. *Next weekend!* She constantly wondered what he was doing, how things were going with his daughter. Was he also seeing another woman there? But what did it matter? She didn't possess him. After all, she had Nate to help her, keep her company, entertain her. What's fair is fair.

Still, as Noelle lay exhausted and alone in her bedroom with the jasmine fragrance drifting in the windows, she thought of Philippe. *Intrepid. Unassailable. Secure.* Granted, she might not possess him, but he certainly possessed her mind. She imagined his cool kisses soothing her burning skin, his warm, strong hands touching her, his strength surrounding her . . . entering her.

Again, sleep was elusive.

It was nearly dusk Sunday evening when Noelle finished painting. She stood back and admired her work. The bed had a wonderfully old-fashioned wicker headboard that she had fallen in love with immediately. Tina was right. All it needed was a coat of white paint. Very nice, she thought, pleased with herself.

She carried her various supplies of brushes and cans and newspapers to the kitchen sink. Before she could wash all the paint off her fingers she heard the rumble of footsteps on the stairs that led to her door. *Nate! Oh, no!* was her first, unavoidable reaction. But courtesy impelled her to answer the rather impatient trio of knocks on the door.

"Philippe!" Her face exuded surprised delight at the sight of him. "You're back! So soon?"

"Obviously," he smiled warmly. "Are you going to stand there gaping at me, or can I come in? You've been busy, and I'd like to see what you've

56

done while I was gone. I have a stake in this place, you know."

"Oh, sure! Of course! Please, come in." Noelle stepped back, allowing his entry.

Philippe closed the door behind him and gazed at her appreciably for a few moments. "Is this any way to greet someone who just traveled three hundred and fifty miles to see you?" he asked as his arms swept around her. He pulled her breathtakingly close and easily lifted her off the floor. His lips met hers in a fierce proclamation of his affection.

He raised his head finally, and smoky brown eyes smoldered with desire. "What's this?" His finger tapped her nose and wiped away a smudge of white paint.

His closeness created a feeling of flushed excitement deep within her as Noelle looked up into his eyes. "I've been painting. The bed. Would you like to see it?" Suddenly she realized how ridiculous she sounded.

He grinned devilishly. "I like your suggestions. Would you like to show it to me?"

"Yes, well, I, uh, just finished it and it looks . . . nice."

He pursed his lips. "Well, then, I'm game. Show me your bed."

"Philippe . . ." She stood, unmoving, her eyes meeting his.

He stepped closer. "I'll just look. Promise."

"Philippe, I didn't mean, that is—"

"I know what you meant. You want to show me

57

your bed. And if look is all you want me to do, then I'll look. Did I tell you I missed you?" Philippe took another small step and enclosed her in his arms tenderly. His lips crushed hers, again kissing them.

In an unavoidable response, Noelle's arms reached around his waist, clinging to him for the strength to stand as an unaccustomed weakness spread through her. Involuntarily, her lips opened, inviting his thrusting tongue. The touch sent spirals of delight bursting inside her and she wanted him with a wild, burning desire. Wanted him far more than she ever had in their youth. For now her desires were those of an adult, experienced and intent, yearning for this man who held her so forcefully. Intrepid. Powerful. Painful. A vague message of discomfort traveled to her languid, desire-drenched brain.

He sighed and lifted his head. "Oh, Noelle, I missed this. Missed you."

She struggled against his grip. "You're . . . you're crushing me!"

He released his hold immediately. "Sorry, I—"

"I know, you don't realize your own brute strength," Noelle finished sarcastically as she rubbed her forearms.

He laughed and caressed her cheek with his finger. "Something like that."

Her hands reached for his shoulders, then trailed longingly down the muscles in his arms. "You *are* strong, Philippe. I don't remember these bulges."

His hands cupped her face and he kissed her nose

and lips affectionately. With a guttural chuckle he bantered, "I won't touch that one, Noelle. I'll only say that most of the bulges are the result of lifting weights, *ma chérie.*"

"Philippe!" she blushed. "Weights?"

"Sure. I had to find a way to compensate for this weak leg. There are things I can't do because of it, like dancing and running. But, rest assured, everything else is in perfect working order! The weights improve muscle tone, not bulges. You should try it sometime, Noelle," he said, an amused smile on his face as he inspected her trim body.

"Me?" She laughed at the idea.

"Of course," he chuckled. "It will help you firm up certain areas, *ma chérie!*" His large hands cupped her breasts and lifted them gently.

She brushed his hands away. "Those are not muscles, sir!"

He shrugged. "Some things can't be improved."

"That's exactly right, Mr. Muscle," she rebuffed. "Besides, I'm so tired tonight, I can hardly lift my head, much less a barbell! Did I ask you why you're back so early? I didn't expect you tonight." She stepped into the living room, and he followed her.

"I had a hell of a week. I was unbelievably busy finalizing the June shipments. Then, Marion, my former wife, and I had an argument Saturday. I had planned to spend all day at Astroworld with Rose. But even that was a disaster. She's been three times. Finally, when my daughter whined to go back home, I realized it was futile. All I could think of was getting back . . . to you."

"I'm glad you came, Philippe. I've—I've missed you too. Let me show you what we've done to the place since you've been gone." Noelle took his hand and led him into the large room that was a combination living room and kitchen.

"Does this tour include showing me the bed?"

"No. Yes! But, you need to realize that the paint's still wet on the headboard! In fact, I planned to sleep on the sofa tonight because the paint smell is too strong in the bedroom."

"I'm adaptable to sofas," he hinted with a smile.

"My sofa's very narrow. And there's room for only one."

"Closeness is one of my specialties. Closeness with you. Noelle, you're why I hurried home."

"Philippe, please, I want . . . I want this to be right. Don't rush it with us."

"I want it to be perfect too. I think it can be, if you give us a chance. How about the floor?"

She laughed and shook her head. "I don't want to ruin our chances, Philippe. But, it . . . it's been so long, and we need to have time to know each other again."

"Sometimes I feel like time is my enemy, Noelle. I have wasted so much of my life without you."

She turned to him with a generous smile and took his hand again. "Come on, Philippe. Don't be so serious. How do you like the new look to my apartment?"

"I like it very much. It looks a lot like you. Fresh and clean and . . . pretty." He admired the brightly colored cushions that accented the white wicker furniture.

"Of course, I have a lot of work yet to do, but I'm very pleased with it. And I have you to thank."

"Who, me? I had nothing to do with all this. I just steered you this way."

"More than that. Why, your men helped move me in. I do appreciate that, Philippe. Everyone has been just wonderful. The only thing I need now is a job."

He walked around the room, hands on his trim waist. "I take it you didn't get the teaching job."

Noelle shook her head. "It was already filled. Now I have to start all over. Come on. See how the bedroom looks with furniture in it. I think you'll like it." She led the way into the other room.

He followed, murmuring, "I know I will."

As they entered the bedroom, a tremendous wailing, much like an infant's cry, pierced the air and Philippe started. "What the hell—"

"Oh, Louie, hush! Everything's okay. Come here." Noelle hurried to the gray cat that arched angrily in the corner, hissing and howling. She reached for him, but he evaded her grasp and fled to the opposite corner, where he continued the same furious argument, feline-style.

"Don't worry about him, Philippe." Noelle smiled. "He's just jealous. Doesn't like men. And it's not just you. He never did like my husband."

"Does this mean your bedroom is off-limits?" Philippe cast a baleful glance at the cat.

"I'll take care of Louie. Don't worry, Philippe." She shooed the angry cat from the room.

"Can I help it if I can't bear to be separated from you again?" His arm caught her around the waist and pulled her against him. "Tonight, Noelle. I've been thinking about nothing but you all weekend."

She straightened up slightly. "Philippe, let's slow down. I think you're pushing me too fast. I—I need more time."

Quietly he gazed into her eyes. "We've lost too much time, Noelle. Why are you being as skittish as your damned cat? We're both adults. You want me as much as I want you. Admit it."

I do, Philippe, she pledged silently. *I do.* Noelle wildly cast about for some way to divert Philippe, knowing only too well how close she was to surrendering to his powerful charm. "Have you eaten?" she blurted out, realizing immediately how ridiculous she sounded. "Let's fix a bite. It'll be the apartment's initiation. I haven't had a chance to cook anything here yet."

"Changing the subject, eh, Noelle?" he laughed, releasing her from his grip.

She took his hand and admitted with a smile, "Just buying a little time. Please understand. This afternoon Aunt Donda sent up some fabulous gumbo that she made. She called it lagniappe."

Philippe smiled gently and decided to go along

with her time-buying. "The old Creole custom of throwing in something for good measure."

"I really like her, Philippe. I'm glad you brought me here."

Together they warmed the gumbo and brewed strong Louisiana coffee. They sat on the sofa before the large window and talked while they ate. There was an easy, relaxed atmosphere between them. The intense sexual charge, so overwhelming before, now seemed subdued, manageable. Noelle felt comfortable and secure. It was just like old times, she mused as she sipped her coffee and gazed dreamily into Philippe's brown eyes.

"Sorry you had such a miserable time in Houston with your daughter, Philippe."

"I just don't know what's wrong. We can't seem to hit it off. I think I need some advice from a woman. I just don't understand Rose. I feel as though a strange little girl in Houston calls me Daddy. She's a part of me, and yet I really don't know her. And she sure as hell doesn't know me!"

Noelle's heart wrenched at his poignant words. It wasn't easy to be a long-distance father, and Philippe seemed so torn by the frustrations of his situation. "Do you always go to Houston to see her?"

He nodded. "Yes. I've never brought her here. She was always too young. Marion didn't think I could manage a small child. And I guess I agreed."

"Well, if she's eight years old, I think she's old enough to come visit her father. And just look at all the wonderful times you could have together here in New Orleans."

"You're right, Noelle. I should bring her here one weekend. That's a good idea."

"I'm a teacher, remember? My work has kept me close to young people. I hope I've learned a little something about them after all those years."

"Do you like it? Teaching?"

"Oh, yes! I love it!" Noelle began enthusiastically. "It's the perfect job. Being with kids is such fun. It keeps me in touch with the joys of simple things that we adults often forget. But kids express them honestly."

"Those things are important to you, aren't they, Noelle?"

"Yes, very. I know it sounds hokey, but I like to think I have a role in shaping kids' futures. It's nice to know you've had some positive influence in a child's life."

He grinned broadly. "You're right, it does sound hokey. Frankly, though, I admire you for being able to spend day after day with the little devils. Sometimes children can be frustrating as hell."

"It's the teaching, not the kids that's frustrating. There are lots of pressures. Lots! Each year there's more and more paperwork. You have to answer to your bosses *and* to parents as well as try to teach the kids. And the parents are simply awful to deal with! Many times it's impossible to forget the job at the end of the day. You take so much of it home with you. Maybe too much."

"Sounds tough to me. Have you ever thought of not teaching for a while, Noelle?"

"Oh, sure. I thought about it very seriously the day I decided to come back home to New Orleans. After that food fight I swore I would never teach again. Now I know I have to." Norm's words echoed in her head. *You can't admit defeat. It's like climbing back on a horse that's thrown you.*

"Food fight? What the hell is that?" Philippe laughed.

Noelle smiled and explained about the array of food splattered over each kid, and how she was in charge, and how she lost control, even how she cried. "I can laugh about it now, but it wasn't so funny the day it happened. I—I fell apart in the principal's office. Cried like a baby. That's when I decided I needed to go back home."

Philippe cupped her chin with his hand. "My poor little Cajun baby. I want to make sure nothing like that ever happens to you again." His lips kissed hers lightly. "You're too precious to be so unhappy with your work."

"It's nice to know I have somebody to lean on. Someone who understands. Someone I can talk to . . . someone to advise me."

"My advice would be for you to do something else for a while."

"But, I can't. I'm a teacher."

"You're also an artist."

"I can't make a living by being an artist," she objected.

"You seem to have some ready arguments to all my suggestions. Since you're starting over here in New Orleans, why don't you just do what you want to do? You have no obligations other than to yourself, Noelle. Do something that you've always wanted to do."

"You make it sound so easy, Philippe."

"It is easy. Just do it," he countered simply.

"But, Philippe—"

Her protest was halted by his kiss, warm and all-encompassing. Noelle was immediately catapulted into the sweet sensuous warmth that overwhelmed her with Philippe's every touch. Tiny kisses rained over her, and she turned her face up for his caresses. His mouth sought the hotly pulsating hollow of her neck, then slowly and sensuously made its way to her breasts.

His hands slipped under her loose shirt to embrace her naked breasts. "Ah, beautiful . . ." he murmured and, lowering his lips, kissed the creamy rises. His palms centered over the aroused tips, fingers spread and kneading gently, sending spasms of delight coursing through her body.

"Oh, Philippe, your touch is magic. . . ."

Together, of one mind, they eased onto the sofa as his fingers fumbled at the buttons on her shirt. "Noelle, *ma chérie,* touching you like this drives me crazy. Tell me you want me tonight!" His kisses radiated over her exposed breasts, sending fiery spirals to the center of her femininity.

66

"Yes . . . yes, I do!" she moaned as she arched to meet his searing caresses.

His tongue circled the rosy protrusions of her nipples, persuading them to aching hardness. White teeth closed over the fiery tips, nipping ever so gently on them.

"Oooh, Philippe . . ." She buried her fingers in his curly chestnut hair, relishing his masculine feel.

He moved along her length, stretching his aroused form to meet hers. Kisses interspersed his words. "Noelle, I want you. Now!"

Neither of them noticed the rumble of footsteps on the outside stairs. Both were startled by the loud knock on the door and heads jerked to attention. Their passion cooled quickly as a male voice called Noelle's name.

"Oh, no," she mumbled and struggled to rise.

"Who the hell is that at this hour?" Philippe growled. "What is this, Noelle? Are you expecting someone?"

Noelle's dark eyes mirrored her apology, for she knew. *She knew!* Noelle rose reluctantly from Philippe's arms, hurriedly buttoning her shirt as she crossed the room.

CHAPTER FOUR

Noelle stared numbly up at the tall, handsome figure standing at her door. "What—what are you doing here, Nate?" It was a dumb question. She knew what he wanted!

He raised the dark green bottle in his hand. "Just got off from work. Did you see me on the news tonight? I was driving by and thought we could have a little celebration. Something to do with your new apartment."

"Not tonight, Nate, I have—"

"Didn't see me, huh? You'd better keep up with what's happening in the world. You don't want that pretty little head of yours to get stale inside, do you? And I know you don't want to miss your favorite newscaster." He smiled down at her while stepping brazenly inside. She backed up instinctively.

Noelle could hear him greeting the other man in the room and had a frantic image of Philippe still on the sofa, still aroused. She scrambled to peer around Nate's tall form, fully expecting to see Philippe in prone position. But, surprisingly enough, he, too, was standing.

"Evening, Nate. A little late for you to be 'driving by,' isn't it?" Philippe's voice was a growl.

"Hello, Philippe," Nate enjoined amiably. "My evening is just beginning. Surprised to find *you* so far from the lake district."

The friction in the air was so strong Noelle could almost reach out and touch it. In a desperate attempt to soothe the air, she stammered, "Nate b-brought some wine, Philippe."

"So I see." Philippe stood beside the sofa, making no attempt to offer Nate a seat.

"Sure! Let's celebrate the new apartment! I'll open the wine," Nate offered and walked into the kitchen as if he had been there a hundred times in the past.

Noelle joined Nate in the kitchen, setting out three wineglasses for him to fill. *Oh, God, why me?* she prayed frantically while scrounging in the cabinet for a light snack. She piled pretzels together in a bowl, and took it to the coffee table before Nate had a chance to finish pouring the wine. She wanted to signal her true feelings to Philippe, but, apparently, the weak smile she gave him didn't do the trick. He glared at her with brooding eyes. How could she let him know she didn't want Nate there? That she hadn't invited him.

69

"Can't you get rid of him?" Philippe muttered through clenched teeth.

"Just this one glass of wine, Philippe. Then I'm sure he'll leave. He can see he's interrupting—" She stopped when Nate approached.

But Nate did not leave. He served Philippe with a low grunt, and Noelle with a wink and a smile. "Here's to a great little apartment and a beautiful little gal."

Noelle acknowledged his toast with a modest smile. She brushed her hair back with a nervous hand. Suddenly the room was warm. Stifling, in fact.

Philippe clinked his glass with hers. "To much happiness in all your new endeavors," he mumbled.

Noelle raised her glass valiantly, a warm smile her only thanks to Philippe.

Nate sat near Noelle's chair, reached for a pretzel, and propped his ankle on his knee. Sighing, he leaned back in the green and white chair. Obviously he was settling in. "Noelle, in just the few days since I helped with your move, you've worked wonders on this place. It's very comfortable and inviting."

"I'm glad you like it, Nate." She didn't dare look at Philippe. He would not be delighted to know Nate had helped her move. Oh, why did he have to say that? But she knew why.

"And I like the furniture in this arrangement, don't you, Philippe? This was just one of my contributions, eh, Noelle?"

70

She nodded, wishing she could sink into the carpet. "Um-hum. And a very good one too."

He smiled invitingly. "Glad you appreciate me. Actually, the place has a sort of homey quality now. Very pleasant indeed. After our little fling last night, Noelle, I figured you'd be ready for some quality Chardonnay and a quiet, comfortable evening at home."

Her eyes cut nervously to Philippe and attempted to change the subject. "Yes, how thoughtful, Nate. I'm—I've been painting today, and I *am* somewhat tired tonight."

But Nate would have none of her tactics. "Let me explain, Philippe."

"Please do," Philippe mused, feigning great interest.

Please don't! Noelle begged silently.

But Nate wasn't about to assuage the situation. With a pleased smile he expounded, "I took Noelle for a moonlight sail on the Mississippi last night. It was something else! Wasn't it, Noelle?"

"Uh, yes. Apt description, Nate," she murmured. The last thing in the world she wanted was to tell Philippe about last night's date with Nate. She didn't look at Philippe, but knew he must be quite agitated by now. In a desperate attempt to change the subject, she offered, "How about some music? I unpacked my records today." Before waiting for an answer from either man, she ran to the storage cabinet and began rifling through the albums, choosing a few of her favorites.

71

"How about more wine?" Nate asked. "Philippe? More wine?"

"Sure, why not?" Philippe extended his glass determinedly. He forced his lips into a tight smile. This was getting more involved. *So Noelle was out with Nate last night? And on a goddamn moonlight sail on the Mississippi! Was it possible that she baited me on tonight, knowing all along Nate would come over after work?* The tiger eyes narrowed ominously.

The music, loud and joyous jazz renditions, was Noelle's attempt to alleviate the tension in the room. But it just seemed to create more. For no sooner did Louis Armstrong's trumpet burst forth when Philippe began to find fault in her choices. Never had his countering of her style of music been more pungent.

"It's too loud. How can we talk? Or think?" he grumbled.

"What?" She leaned toward him. *Please understand, Philippe,* her dark eyes begged.

Philippe's voice roared above the pitch of the trumpet. "I said, the volume's a little powerful, isn't it?" *You led me on,* his tiger eyes accused silently.

"Oh, yes. I suppose it is." Noelle rose and fiddled with the stereo again, changing records in the process. *I care for you,* she tried desperately to say with her movements.

"Is that all you have?" It was Philippe again, cold.

She raised her eyebrows. "That's 'Cozy' Cole. I

72

thought you liked him. He was a great drummer." *What's wrong with you tonight?*

He shook his head stubbornly. "Couldn't compare with Shelley Manne." *You're playing games, Noelle.*

"He can compare with anyone in the business! Cole was a versatile drummer!" She realized that she was falling right into Philippe's trap. He wanted to argue. She was all too willing. She set another record on the turntable. *Please, Philippe . . .*

"My God! Who's that? The record sounds ancient!"

"The record *is* old. It's 'Fatha' Hines on the piano. Surely you like *him!*"

"It's an endurance test."

"Damn! So are you! Philippe! I can't believe you're being so pig-headed!" *You're impossible!*

"Sorry, Noelle. You go ahead and listen to whatever you want to. I won't belittle your off-beat taste." *You did this just to aggravate me tonight!*

"We're enjoying this *real,* old-time jazz, aren't we, Nate?" She turned to Nate for support.

Nate smiled and shrugged his hands. "I'm enjoying the show!"

Philippe set his glass down angrily. "Well, I won't be part of this evening's entertainment! Not for you two, anyway. I was just leaving!"

"Philippe—don't go." Noelle realized what was happening and knew she was helpless to stop it. She herself had driven him away. Oh, why did she even open the door to Nate?

73

"Thanks for the wine, Nate," Philippe commented stiff-lipped. Then he turned to Noelle. There was more emotion in his face than just anger. Distrust shone clear and bright in his eyes. "Good evening, Noelle. Be careful that you don't roll off that narrow sofa!" He was out the door before she had a chance to protest.

Distrust! Noelle's heart sank desolately to the pit of her stomach as she listened to the rattle of Philippe's footsteps on the stairs.

Noelle's insomnia plagued her again that night, tired as she was. It wasn't because of Philippe's jealous outburst. Nor did Nate's rude intrusion keep her awake. When she told Nate she was very tired and that she wanted to be alone, he left, almost as angrily as Philippe. However, Nate's feelings weren't her concern. Philippe was the only one she cared for, and she had failed miserably to let him know it. Weary, she just wanted to block out everything and get some sleep.

As she lay alone on the narrow sofa, Philippe's words reverberated in her head. It was the first time anyone had said to her, "Do what you want to do. Whatever makes you happy."

Do what you want to do. It was a spontaneous, free-sounding statement. It was liberating! It was challenging! What *did* she want to do? Besides teaching? Noelle had never seriously considered anything else.

She had always done what was required, what was necessary, what was expected. She had been a good student. It was expected that with her good grades she would be a teacher. Her mother and sister were teachers. And Noelle had all the qualifications of being an excellent teacher. Plus, she loved kids.

But whoever said you have to teach just because you love kids? Noelle wasn't sure who planted that seed, but it had lived inside her for years. And, for years, teaching had been thoroughly satisfying. It was only lately that she had problems with it, or even considered doing something else. But what? It was almost blasphemous to admit dissatisfaction with teaching!

When she graduated from college, teaching degree in hand, she wanted more adventure, more excitement than her hometown could offer and soon left New Orleans. Her sister, Tina, was a newlywed. She and Max were happy, in love, the perfect couple. The heart of the matter, though, was that Noelle felt jilted by a man she loved. *Philippe Merritt.*

Actually Noelle was jilted by a faraway war, by circumstances. When Philippe left her to go to that distant land rather than stay in New Orleans, all she wanted was to get away from everything that reminded her of him. So she answered an ad and escaped to New Jersey. To teach. It was the steady and respectable thing to do.

So was her marriage. There was more expectation and curiosity than love. It was far too late when Noelle realized the only thing she had in common with her husband was teaching. Afterward, she wondered how they had managed to stay together three years.

The divorce, inevitable from the start, spelled failure to Noelle. She couldn't bring herself to tell her family about it for months. For once she was glad to be in New Jersey, far away from their questions and sympathy. She had tried to hold her life together. It was necessary that she "hang in there," build her independence, stay with the system. Noelle believed all of that wholeheartedly. It was what she had been taught. Admittedly she wanted to continue teaching —until the day of the food fight.

That hadn't been the first time she'd been reduced to tears at school. Neither was it the first time Noelle had lost control of a group. However, it was the most explosive. And the most devastating to her self-esteem. On that day, at that moment, she was ready to quit teaching.

Now, though, her views differed, tempered by a few weeks rest and new circumstances. Norm said she must go back to teaching. *Must!* It was necessary, and she agreed. But Philippe, dear, wonderful Philippe, had challenged her when he said *do what you want to do* . . . Well, what *did* she want to do?

In the dusky light of morning Noelle rose and took a warm shower. An idea was beginning to form. She creamed and powdered her slender body, then pulled on her oldest, most faded jeans. The threads were white along the fronts of the thighs, darker blue along the inseam. They were wonderfully comfortable.

The idea grew. She slipped a tube top over her head and looked at herself in the mirror. *Should I go braless? I've never—ever—had the freedom to work braless.*

Yes! I'd like to know what it's like to work naturally, freely! Noelle grabbed a long-sleeved linen shirt. It would protect her from the sun, or if she had a fit of modesty. Gazing again into the mirror, she asked aloud, "Where's that prudish schoolteacher? Not here!" She laughed aloud at herself and slid her feet into blue, thick-soled thongs. Perfect!

Noelle scrounged in the back of the closet. Her tall easel, her box of pastels, paper—what else would she need? Tape! She would need tape. She scrambled in a drawer. Also, she should take along a stool. The kitchen fold-up one would do for today. Armed to the teeth, she maneuvered out the door and down the long stairs.

She giggled with anticipation. This was perfect! It had been her dream since she was a child. It was something she had always wanted to do. It would make her happy.

Jackson Square was just beginning to come to life when she hauled her paraphernalia to the wrought-iron railing surrounding the park. Noelle picked her spot carefully. It had to be perfect, with a view of the church and a glimpse of the river.

Noelle munched a beignet and sipped strong,

black coffee as she set up her easel and stool. She taped a few sketches on the railing. There, now. Her "spot" was beginning to take on the right appearance. And she should look the part too. Bohemian. Free and easy. Comfortable. She started to remove her shirt.

"You're new." The masculine statement startled her.

Noelle automatically pulled the shirt back around her shoulders and wheeled around to face a dark man of about fifty-five who sported a scraggly, grayish beard. "Uh, yes," she admitted, then quickly decided it would be unwise to tell him this was her first day at the square. "New to this side," she added, and gestured to the opposite railing where other artisans were setting up shop.

"Huh," he grunted. "I'm Sam." He stood there, waiting for her response.

Should she give him her real name? She decided against it. "I'm . . . Sarah."

"Sarah, huh?" He pondered a moment before friendly brown eyes warmed with a trace of a smile. "Can you sing like Sarah Vaughan? She's my favorite nightingale."

"No, I can't," Noelle smiled delightedly. "But she's one of my favorites too."

"Too bad. I was hoping we could make some good music today. I usually hold down this corner, here." He shuffled to the spot beside her and opened a metal folding stool.

Music? Noelle glanced curiously at Sam's small case.

"But I see you're an artist," he continued blithely.

"Yes," she admitted proudly. "I'm doing pastel sketches today."

Shaking his grizzled gray head, he muttered, "Too bad. Artists are a dime a dozen."

Noelle spun around angrily. *A dime a dozen!* Damn him, anyway! Just when she was satisfied that this was the perfect job for her, this Sam person shoots her down! Well, what did he know? She raised her chin defiantly. She certainly wouldn't let this man spoil her fun. Her wonderful, perfect job! This was what she wanted to do and she would damn well do it!

She watched through slitted eyes as Sam fitted his trumpet together and blew out the valves. When he began one of her favorite jazz pieces, Noelle knew this would be a day to remember! It turned out to be a week she would never forget!

Noelle didn't hear from Philippe all week. It was just as well. It gave her some time alone to get adjusted to her new job. She became a solicitor, learning quickly how to compete with other "dime-a-dozen" artists on the block. Sam taught her that the sales pitch was the attraction that made the difference. Realistically, though, Noelle knew that sometimes it was her physical appeal in her outfit of tube top and jeans that pulled in the tourists.

She also found it was a physically exhausting job that coupled with a long day spent in the fresh air aided her slumber each night. This was what she had been needing for a long time to cure her insomnia. She certainly didn't take her problems home from this job each night. By the time she ate a bite and showered, she fell into a dead sleep. It was by no means the perfect job, but it gave her a respite from her problems. She knew she would have to deal with them of course, but not now . . . perhaps someday soon.

"Noelle! Is that you? What in hell are you doing here?" Philippe's strong hands gripped her shoulders and shook her slightly.

"Sir," she grated adroitly. "Would you like your portrait in pastels? Something to take home to your girlfriend?"

"Girlfriend!"

Noelle twisted from his grasp, and when he paused momentarily, she pointed to the kitchen stool. "Perhaps one for your daughter. Have a seat."

"Noelle, this is crazy!"

"Have a seat, please!" she advised firmly. "You're taking up someone else's time."

Noelle pushed Philippe to the stool, where he sat impatiently with one leg still on the sidewalk. "Noelle, what in hell are you doing here?" he repeated, loud enough to be heard above the wailing of Sam's horn.

"Sketching you. Sit still!" She worked quickly,

her hand moving from the top to the bottom of the sketch pad.

"But why are you here? I've been trying to get you all week!"

"Why I am here?" she taunted. "Like everyone else, I'm trying to make enough money to pay my bills of course! Why else does one work?"

"But here on the street! It's—it's just not where you should be. It's dangerous!" He gestured frustratedly and her eyes caught the strength in those arms. The strength she longed for, yet had not felt all week.

"It's better than some street jobs I can think of! Besides, this isn't dangerous! It's been fun! And Sam, here, has kept an eye on me all week."

"I'll bet he's not the only one either," Philippe scoffed. "Trouble is, he couldn't hear if you screamed your head off, for all the noise from that damned horn!"

"He doesn't need to hear me. I'm perfectly fine. Turn your head a little to the left." She scaled his angular face to her thumb and sketched quickly, trying to quell the deep desire to reach out and touch the rugged features she was drawing.

Strains of "When the Saints Come Marching In" quieted, and Philippe's voice lowered to a more reasonable tone. "Noelle, you haven't answered my question. Why are you here? Doing this?"

"Actually, it was your idea, Philippe." She smiled generously. "And I want to thank you. It's been a lovely experience."

"Mine?" He was aghast. "How is that possible? I've been out of town all week. Maybe you're getting me confused with your tall friend."

"Nate? Oh, no," she chuckled. "You said it the last evening we spent together, before Nate arrived. Remember?" Her dark eyes pinned him to the stool.

"Said what?"

"You said, 'Do what you want to do.' Well, ever since I was a little girl I've wanted to be a street artist. It just intrigued me somehow. Your suggestion gave me the impetus to try it. After all, I wasn't doing anything else this week." She shrugged and the frustrations she felt were embodied in the tired movement of those thin shoulders.

"Noelle, darling!" Immediately Philippe was beside her, cradling her face tenderly in his large hands. "I wish I'd known you'd take my words so seriously. I've been worried to death about you all week. I finally called Tina and couldn't believe my ears when she told me you were here. You look exhausted." His thumbs gently caressed the faint blue semi-circles under her eyes. "What's this? Still not sleeping?"

She shook her head. "Oh, yes. Better this week than in a long time. I'm just a little tired today. I have to get up very early to cinch my spot."

"It hurts me to see you like this. Come on, we're going home."

She gestured toward her sketch pad. "I can't leave yet, Philippe. It isn't even dark."

His arm clamped around her like iron. "Oh, yes, you can. I'm taking you right now."

"Philippe—"

His eyes settled evenly on her. "We'll discuss this, and other things, at home. Come on." He began to gather her things, and Noelle slowly followed suit. The fight in her was gone.

She *was* tired. And perhaps she did want to end this exhausting, but satisfying week and go home with Philippe.

As they left Sam to hold down the corner position by himself, Philippe wrapped his free arm solidly around Noelle. He assured her in a low tone, meant just for her, "I'm taking you home for dinner, a warm bath, and bed—and not necessarily in that order."

CHAPTER FIVE

Noelle was too exhausted to object further to Philippe's sweet demands to go home. Frankly it sounded like a marvelous idea. She accompanied him without objection, sinking behind the steering wheel of her car while he dumped her paraphernalia in the backseat. Her ugly green VW followed his sleek gray Mercedes across town, weaving around traffic and trolley cars to the gracious two-story house whose attic she now called home.

Of all her recent ventures, the move to this little apartment was the best. In her heart Noelle was sure of it, even though there were times when she doubted all her other actions, including the decision to leave New Jersey. The job search in New Orleans just wasn't working out.

She hated to admit it, but she had even considered returning to Jersey. At least she had work experience and acquaintances there and, inevitably, more chance of getting another job. She could always go back to Norm and Grace B. Shackle Junior High. A chilling shudder ripped through her warm, perspiring body at the mere thought. *No! It'll work out here! It just has to! I couldn't stand to go back!*

Together she and Philippe hauled her equipment up the back stairs. Noelle reached for her key and placed it in Philippe's outstretched palm. Her fingers caressed his, the nails scraping across the center of his hand. Her eyes rose to meet his, and she felt, rather than saw, his concerned gaze. He seemed to radiate more emotion than she had ever dreamed was possible. In the angled lines of his face was the concern, the strength, the love, she had needed from Philippe for years. *Love?* She quivered with anticipation.

He made her feel important. *Intrepid. Invincible.* How could one look give her all that? Noelle wasn't sure, but Philippe's message was clear. His irresistible eyes spoke of love! Desire was obvious in those tiger eyes. In Noelle's expression was an unmistakable response: *Yes!*

He tore away from their locked gaze. With a jerky motion Philippe grasped the key from her and fitted it into the slot. Stepping inside, he flipped on the light nearest the door, then directed her, "You take a nice, warm bath, Noelle. I'll fix supper."

Noelle nodded and complied, as if it were the most natural thing in the world for her to do. Halfway across the room she halted and turned around to look at him. "Philippe?" Her voice was suddenly

85

raspy, emotional, matching her gritty, tired body. "Thank you for . . ."

"For what?" He shrugged.

She swallowed tightly. "For being there when I needed you. And, for—everything."

His eyes softened. "It's the very least I can do for my little Cajun baby. I want . . . I want to see you happy. You'd better wait until you've eaten my cooking before you thank me though."

"I'm happy tonight, Philippe," she avowed before heading toward her bedroom.

In the quiet privacy of her room, Noelle could hear Philippe rattling pans in the kitchen as she stripped off her grimy clothes. Louie gazed disdainfully at her through his cool green cat eyes and finally rose to wind seductively around her bare legs. He skittered away when she adjusted the nozzle and the shower sent forth a noisy blast of water. Standing zombielike under the flow, she allowed the tepid water to surge over the top of her head and trickle down the entire length of her body.

God! It felt fantastic. It was a psychological relief to wash away the dirt and imagine it, along with all her troubles, flowing down the drain. It felt good to know that Philippe was in the other room preparing supper. Caring. She needed him to show her that he cared, to take care of her. But, especially, she needed to have him in her little attic home tonight. This was exactly the way it should be. A dream come true.

Noelle toweled her thick, dark hair, feeling relaxed and content. She hesitated only a moment before slipping into her favorite cotton robe, the one that reminded her of Louisiana. She smiled as she combed through thick curls, letting them fall naturally around her face and on her shoulders.

She emerged refreshed and generally tranquil. "What are you cooking out here, Philippe? It smells marvelous!"

Philippe smiled with masculine satisfaction as she appeared. "Why, thank you, madame. And you look scrumptious, even in that gawdy, audacious robe!" He punctuated his statement with a kiss on her forehead to soften its blow.

However, Noelle was in no mood to let his remarks faze her. She pirouetted before him, allowing a full three-hundred-sixty-degree view of the bold pink and white flowers set on brilliant green leaves that were imprinted on the robe. "Audacious? Don't you like my lush robe? When I saw it on sale back in New Jersey, I grabbed it up on the spot. It reminded me of home and I like it. Besides, it's the most comfortable thing I own!"

He eyed her attire with shrewd evaluation. "I daresay, you're the only one on either side of the Mississippi who would consider buying it. You're lovely in it, baby. But then, you're lovely in anything. Or nothing!" He swatted her playfully on the bottom.

"I don't care what you think of it," she answered indignantly. "Everyone has one or two items in their wardrobe that are classified as 'most comfortable.' And this is mine. Now, what have we here?" She inhaled the aroma as she lifted the lid on the skillet. "Ahh! Everything! Onions, ham, green peppers, mushrooms, cheese . . . wow!"

"You must be a gourmet cook, Noelle. This is a very well-stocked kitchen. I just used a little of everything I found in your pantry."

"Oh, Philippe, I didn't know you were so talented!"

He twirled the spatula with semi-expert grace, making the most of his dramatic flair. "Aw, shucks, ma'am. It ain't nothin'. Just the greatest li'l omelet in the world!"

"You've convinced me! Looks terrific and smells even better! I'm starved! Let's eat!" Noelle reached for plates and handed them to Philippe. "You serve, since you obviously are the superior cook here."

He served them both with comical sophistication, drawing more laughter from her. "The only thing missing is the *vino*. A little Chablis helps even the best omelet. Where should I look, Noelle?"

"Wine? With an omelet?"

"You question zee chef?" He glared unsmilingly. She shrugged and opened a cabinet. "My wine stock is quite low, Chef Merritt, but we'll see what's here. Ahhhh! Here is the wine that Nate left."

Philippe smiled devilishly and poured two small glasses of wine. "Then, by all means, let's partake. Nate is so generous to leave his 'quality Chardonnay' for us to enjoy!"

Noelle laughed aloud. "Nate would be furious if

he thought you and I were enjoying the last of his wine!" They toasted each other smilingly and hooked their arms gaily for the first sip.

Philippe's eyes met hers and his smile faded momentarily. His gaze dropped to her lips, then he nodded abruptly and handed her his crystal glass. "You take care of the wine, and I'll bring the plates."

They sat on the sofa, thighs touching, close enough to be intimate. It was pleasant and no one spoke for a few minutes. Noelle tucked her feet underneath and ate half her serving before commenting, "Philippe, this is just great. Where did you learn to prepare such a fantastic omelet?"

"Oh, we bachelors learn a few simple tricks in the kitchen, then stick with them until they're perfected. I've probably fixed a million of these over the years. No, two million." He laughed and lines crinkled around his tiger eyes.

"Well, you've got this one down pat. It's wonderful. Thank you. It's just what I needed tonight."

"I had to do something to make up for the ridiculous way I behaved the other night. Sorry about that, Noelle. I was just—"

"Jealous," she finished with a definite teasing twinkle in her eyes. "I won't forgive you so easily for abandoning me with Nate!"

He reached for her hand and brought it to his lips. "It seemed pretty damn clear that the two of you wanted to be alone. Damned right, I'm jealous! I can't stand the thought of another man with you. I know it's unreasonable, Noelle. But when Nate said you two had been together all week, I just went crazy inside." His lips brushed her knuckles sensuously. "His insinuations drove me wild."

"Philippe, that's all it was. Insinuations. Whatever message you received was garbled. There is nothing between Nate and me. Surely you know that. I didn't know he was coming over that night. Nor did I want him here. Interrupting us."

"Nothing between you?" he repeated as if for confirmation. His kisses brushed each finger and the electricity that had charged between them all evening began to flow through her veins. His warm touch and gentle kiss were full of fire. Noelle longed for more.

"Absolutely nothing. Nate and I don't . . . just don't fit."

Philippe kissed the pulse point on her wrist, then raised his head curiously. "Don't fit? What the hell are you talking about?"

"Nate's too tall for me. We don't fit easily. He—I can't even dance with him. My fingers go to sleep from reaching up all the time." She smiled jauntily and traced his lower lip. "But with us, Philippe, it's different."

Philippe tugged possessively on her arm and she came willingly into his arms. "Do we fit, Noelle?" His eyes caressed her face and lingered on her lips.

"Perfectly." She smiled and placed her hand on his cheek.

Her thumb rubbed his lower lip as she applied

tender pressure to bring his face closer. His lips rained zephyrlike kisses from her lips to her closed eyelids. Sliding her hand to the warmth of his neck, she could feel the pulsing power there as his kiss deepened. Her fingers eased gently around his heated neck until they nestled in the brown curls at his nape.

"Oh, Philippe . . ."

"God, Noelle, do you know what you do to me?"

"I have an idea," she admitted softly. "And I'm glad. I'd hate to think I was the only one who felt this way." She snuggled against his chest, laying her head against his shoulder. "I was so pleased to see you this evening, Philippe. So grateful to hear you say, 'Let's go home.' We belong here together."

His hand caressed her dark curls lovingly, and his voice was thick and rough. "You had me worried this week. After the unpleasantness with Nate I was jealous as hell. Then I had to go out of town and couldn't reach you. Do me a favor, please."

"What?"

"Get a telephone!" His tone was a gruff command, teasing, yet somber.

She shrugged lightly. "That is one luxury that will have to wait until the job comes along."

He studied her words briefly, then without comment continued. "Finally I called Tina. It occurred to me that you might consider going back to Jersey. That was a frightening thought."

She was startled by his insight, but objected stoutly, convincing herself as well. "Oh, no! I won't go back, Philippe. I'm here to stay. This is where I belong."

His arm shifted her tightly against his chest. *"This* is where you belong. Here in my arms. But, why, for God's sake, did you go down to the park to work all week? Whatever made you do that?"

"I told you, Philippe. You gave me the idea!" Noelle sat upright and smiled happily.

"Me? But how?"

"You made me realize just how much some of my decisions had been influenced by other people. Before Nate came, and we were talking, you said, 'Do what you want to do.' Those words were like magic to me! I couldn't get them out of my head! I suppose everyone should have the opportunity to do what they really want to do at some point in their lives. Well, since I was a little child, I have wanted to be a street artist on Jackson Square. It has always been my dream."

"Why? What is so appealing about being a street artist?" He looked at her incredulously. Noelle could tell from Philippe's expression that he couldn't understand her motives.

She tried to explain, as well as understand, herself. "Oh, I don't know. I guess for some of the same reasons that make people want to run their own business. It looked like so much fun and so free, and I was intrigued with the idea of looking at someone and completing a sketch right then and there. Now, with me out of work, seemed to be a good time to try it. I thought . . ." She laughed softly at her misconceptions. "I thought it would be the perfect job. Drawing, working with people out in the fresh air, making them happy, and dressing casually are all things I love. Sounded perfect to me."

"And is it?" His finger lightly traced a line from her cheek to the pulse in her neck.

"I failed to take into consideration the brutal fact that I can't live on the earnings of such a great job. Not if I want to continue eating!"

"Sometimes money isn't the most important factor in a job," Philippe mused.

"No," she admitted. "But it is necessary for certain habits I've developed. Like eating and living under a roof. I've had my fling with a fantasy. Now I'm ready to get down to business. Next week I'll be back to pounding the schoolyards for a job. Teaching is what I should be doing. Besides, the street was very hot, and I had to coat my nose with zinc the last three days to keep it from burning. Can you imagine what I would look like by the end of this summer? Burnt toast!"

"Ah-ha, so you are willing to concede that this new effort has its drawbacks?"

She nodded sheepishly. "I can admit it. Plus, the street is a very dirty and noisy place. Actually, noisy is putting it mildly. If I hear 'Saints' one more time this year, I think I'll scream!"

Philippe laughed delightedly. "That's quite an admission, coming from a die-hard, Dixieland jazz enthusiast!"

She reached down to rub the calf of one leg. "Well, this enthusiast is very tired tonight. My legs are killing me. I'm just not cut out for this job of standing on my feet all day, every day."

"I'll give you a massage, Noelle." His suggestion was made as if he were offering a simple glass of water.

"A massage?" She swallowed, the thoughts of his hands on her sending nervous spirals of heat vibrating through her.

"Sure. I'm a very good masseur. Learned it from an Oriental nurse in one of the numerous hospitals I inhabited on my way home from Nam. It's one means of relieving the pain, and, in many ways, better than drugs. Let me help you relax, Noelle."

It stabbed her inside to hear of his pain, although she knew it had to have been a reality. "Was it bad, Philippe? The pain?"

"Six surgeries on this leg. One on my back. Rehabilitation for a full year. It was hell." He said it so matter-of-factly, it could have been a weather report.

"Oh, Philippe, I'm so sorry," she murmured softly and pulled his lips to meet hers in a gentle kiss.

"Are you going to let me do this massage?" His voice was low.

"Yes," she whispered. The thought of Philippe's hands moving over her was too thrilling to avoid. Her heart tripled its beats. A massage from Philippe sounded heavenly!

"First, I need some oil. Something to help my hands slide easily."

"Baby oil is all I have."

He smiled and led her through the living room. "That'll be fine for my little Cajun baby."

She padded into her bedroom and knelt to dig into one of the boxes still packed from the move. When Noelle finally found the bottle of baby oil, she stood to find Philippe turning the radio dial.

Over his shoulder he ordered, "Get rid of that damned cat. Apparently, he and I can't share the same bedroom. Then lie down. And that awful robe has to go."

Soft, soothing music filled the background. She looked accusingly at the radio.

"Just a little relaxing music to set the mood," he murmured.

Noelle slid a hand around Louie, who was pacing the length of her bed, agitated by the presence of Philippe in his domicile. Now, however, even the cat seemed aware that this had become Philippe's domain. She dumped the cat unceremoniously out the door, then secured the lock. Looking back at Philippe, their eyes met.

Noelle's eyes traveled from the freshly painted white rattan bed with its new, quilted coverlet back to Philippe's brown eyes. It was an awkward moment. "I—I'll get a towel so the . . . oil won't get on my new coverlet." She stumbled to the bathroom and brought back a thick, aquamarine towel. Philippe had pulled the coverlet back and folded it neatly at the foot of the bed.

"We don't want to ruin the cover," he explained. "At least the sheets are washable."

"Yes," she mumbled and spread her towel.

"Lie down on your stomach and get comfortable," he instructed.

Noelle nodded, her eyes lowering to the towel.

"Without the robe—"

"Just a minute." She disappeared again in the bathroom and emerged without the robe. A matching aquamarine towel was wrapped modestly around her, tucked high under each arm. "Now." She quickly positioned herself on the bed.

Philippe's warm hands adjusted her arms, then moved to her head. Fingers spread wide, he buried them in her thick hair, kneading her tense scalp, moving her head from side to side. Fingertip pressure was applied to her temples and all across her forehead, then each step was retraced.

His voice was low and hypnotic. "Just relax. Imagine yourself floating in the warm Gulf Stream. The waves are gently rocking you back and forth. You are warm and very comfortable. Rocking back and forth. The breeze is cool. The water is taking you to a sunny, beautiful place full of flowers and nice breezes."

As Philippe's voice soothed and mesmerized her, Noelle could feel the tension easing away, sliding all the way down to her toes and out of her body. When his hands touched her shoulders, they were

96

warm and slick from the oil. Or was the heat coming from her own skin?

Noelle was floating, free and easy, loose and relaxed. Only Philippe's hands were there to guide the way. She was never out of his reach, her skin responding to his every manipulation.

Long, strong fingers encircled her neck, fingertips pressing tiny circles of delight into her. A soft moan escaped her lips quite unconsciously.

His hands froze. "Am I hurting you?"

"Noooo, it's nice," she sighed. "So nice . . ."

His hands continued down her inert form. The muscles in her shoulders were rendered into soft putty, melting into submission along with her will. Each vertebra along her back received individual attention, and when he reached the aquamarine towel, it quickly became a small strip across her buttocks, but she hardly noticed.

He followed the curve of her backbone all the way to the base of her spine with his slick, strong fingers, touching every part of her with practiced skill, gently, but firmly. Suddenly the towel was gone. Fitting his palms over her rounded buttock muscles, he massaged and kneaded, enflaming more than Noelle's skin. Spires of sensual frenzy rose inside her and each thrust of his hands became fuel for the fire kindling in the deepest part of her.

In a futile effort to control her raging passion and wild imagination, Noelle spoke. "Philippe, I told you about my dreams and doing what I've always wanted to do. What about your dreams? Are you happy now?"

His hands crawled agonizingly along her ribs and the sides of her breasts, creating havoc with her senses. "If you mean happy with my work, the answer is yes. I'm doing what I've always known I would do. But, my secret dreams, Noelle, always included you."

"Me?" The word was a surprised little gasp as he shifted her legs apart and began to vigorously massage the muscles. His touch became increasingly intimate as he grasped her sensitive inner thigh, driving her crazy with desire.

"I've wanted you for longer than I care to remember, Noelle. Far longer than I should. You were my dream lover, my little Cajun baby." He lingered longer on her thigh, then finally, he moved down to her calf and she breathed again.

"Philippe, don't say that!"

He rubbed each foot, every toe, until her legs and feet tingled. "Noelle, *ma chérie,* there were times when I was in pain, far from home, for months at a time. Something, someone, had to keep me going. You were my incentive."

"But Philippe, you had a wife. And a child."

His hands retraced the sensuous trails he had previously created, caressing their way back up her slick form. When did his touch change from the firm businesslike grip of the masseur to the erotic stroking of a lover? His right hand slid around her waist, under her.

"Yes, I did. But Marion could never offer what I needed. Your image did." His hands eased up to hold her flattened breasts, massaging the hardening nipples erotically. His voice was low. "I imagined you like this, Noelle. Dreamed of making love to you. There were times when those thoughts were all that kept me going."

"Philippe . . . Philippe, I don't know what to say. I had no idea."

"Don't say anything. Just enjoy." One hand moved down past her ribs, her belly, to the crest of her femininity. She lay on his hand, unavoidably applying pressure. His fingers stroked and massaged against her natural insistence, finally slipping to the heart of her desires. She arched to meet his rhythmic caresses.

"Noelle, make my dreams come true," he urged hoarsely. "Let me hold you. I want to make love to you."

As if in a trance, she turned over. It seemed perfectly natural to be here with Philippe, his hand still caressing her. She knew that they would be lovers tonight. It was something she wanted now, had wanted for years. Perhaps he had been her dream lover too. He was perfect in her memory, someone who could fill every empty void in her life.

Without a word he bent to kiss the creamy flesh of her breasts. The touch of his lips sent flames of fiery passion through her veins, passion that had been dormant too long. She breathed deeply and closed her eyes ecstatically as his insistent lips closed over each dark aureole, pulling gently. Then his soft lips circled the swollen breasts, until she yearned for a stronger touch.

A soft sound escaped her lips as his tongue coaxed each nipple to an aching hardness. He kissed a hot trail between her now-heaving breasts, up her pale neck, to her waiting lips. His kiss, always gentle and persuasive, was now passionate and strong. She opened her lips to his thrusting tongue, the motion matching that of his hand.

Instinctively, Noelle curved aggressively to his touch. The repeating moan she heard was her own as Philippe's skillful stimulation increased to an almost unbearable torment. His kisses again sought her breasts and Noelle's hands became lost in his brown hair, pulling him to her vigorously.

"Ah, Noelle, you're so beautiful. So responsive . . ." His voice trailed away as his kisses tantalized her stomach and navel.

"Philippe, come to me," she gasped in a strained voice. "I want you."

His tongue circled her lower belly maddeningly, then followed his stroking fingers along her inner thighs. She opened her limbs to his gentle probing, writhing with spasms of delight. Suddenly she shuddered as climactic waves surged through her body.

Philippe held her tightly, caressing and murmuring words of love. Then he unbuttoned his shirt with one hand and shed his clothes quickly. Gently he brought her again to the brink of ecstasy. Her torturous wait for him was brief, and she felt his aroused masculine frame molded strongly to her soft femininity. Their coming together was wild and wonderful, long-delayed by years and circumstances beyond their control.

There was no hesitation as, with relentless desire, he entered her, creating such an impassioned response that her fingers dug savagely into his back. Shock waves united them in a mutual rhythm of inexhaustible desire as they exploded together. Noelle wished this wonderful paradise of passion between them could last forever.

Their lovemaking was frenzied, passionate, fueled by a desperate need to realize lost dreams, to make up for lost time, to possess totally and completely. The impact of their lovemaking was stronger, more dynamic, more satisfying than either of them could ever have dreamed.

"I never . . . want this . . . to end," she murmured breathlessly.

"It's just the beginning for us, baby," he assured her.

"I mean now, Philippe," she wiggled passionately against him. "This is so . . . good . . ."

"It can happen again, *ma belle*. Right now. Just rock against me." His hand slid under her hips, guiding her expertly. Within moments Noelle was shuddering again to the rhythm Philippe had created.

"Oh, Philippe," she breathed. "I've never done that before."

He kissed her damp temple and pushed her dark

hair back. "I told you, we've just begun, Noelle. Look at what we've missed. Both of us."

Her hands cradled his face and she kissed him. "I've missed so much by not having you, Philippe. Oh, I want to press you to me so you can never leave!" Her hands wrapped around his ribs tightly, then moved down to stroke his hips while he was still a part of her.

Abruptly her right hand halted, frozen to the shape of his hip beneath her fingers. "Philippe? Oh, my God, Philippe! What—"

"It's a scar, Noelle." His tone was suddenly hard. "Please, don't touch it."

CHAPTER SIX

"Philippe, oh Philippe . . ." Noelle's voice was a shocked gasp as her hand brushed tenderly over the scar-roughened skin on his hip. The line was deep and sunken, evolving to a hard ridge along his thigh. Her fingers explored its length.

"Old war wounds," he mumbled, his tone lightening. He kissed her earlobe and shifted to the side.

"Don't—don't try to make jokes. Does it hurt?" Her hand remained gently on the scars.

"Not now. It's completely healed, although sometimes sensitive to the weather. I can usually predict rain," he chuckled.

But Noelle was in no mood for humor. "Oh, God, Philippe. I'm—I'm so sorry. I was here in the States, safe from harm, and you were going through this hell. I feel so guilty. My biggest worries were dealing with discipline in the classroom and lesson plans, while you were struggling to walk."

He nestled her against his ample chest. "First, I was struggling to survive, *ma belle.* Then came walking."

She caressed the leg, her touch expressing more than words ever could. "You . . . you nearly died?" Just saying it was painful, horrifying. "I feel so . . . so ashamed. I never realized—"

"I don't want to dwell on the past. It's something I've got to live with; that's all. At least I came out alive. All that is over, Noelle. What's most important to me is what's happening now. You and me. Just us. You are still my dear, sweet Cajun baby. I've waited for this night for ten years. Dreamed about it. You'll never know the times I thought of you when . . . when maybe I shouldn't."

"While you were still married?"

"Yes," his voice rumbled from his chest. "Marion and I didn't have much of a marriage. We both went into it with false expectations. I wanted someone with your vitality and spirit. She expected an easier life, not so many problems, more wealth."

"But your family had the big rice farm."

He shrugged and Noelle could feel the ripple of rugged muscles on which she lay. "Once Marion was a part of the family she knew there was little value in the farm's business. My father wasn't far-sighted enough to expand our assets and, while I was in Nam, the whole thing fell apart. She tried to work there with my father, but that was a disaster. Then the problems really started."

"You came back from Vietnam injured," Noelle

concluded and ran her hand purposely over his taut belly and back to the rough scars.

Philippe shivered at her sensuous touch. "That was only a part of it. In all fairness to Marion, they were horrible years. First, my older brother was killed overseas. That was . . . very bad." He paused and Noelle could tell that his words were an understatement. He continued painfully. "Before our family could reckon with the tragedy of losing Dominic in this hellish war, they sent me home, injured and facing more surgery. They said I would never walk again. All this was too much for my father. A heart attack killed him. I began to handle the business from a hospital bed, finally graduating to a wheelchair, then crutches. It wasn't much of a life for a young wife."

"You can't blame yourself for what happened to your family, Philippe. And, the injury certainly wasn't your doing! Couldn't Marion see that you were only doing what you had to do under the circumstances?"

"She saw what she wanted to see. However, there was one thing she definitely could blame me for. Her pregnancy. And she did. She decided to return to her family in Houston to have the baby. I was served divorce papers from there."

"How unfair!"

"Well, Marion felt that life with me had been terribly unfair. Maybe she was right. At any rate, she couldn't bear to stick around for more. Can't say that I blame her. Things were pretty bleak around here. The rice farm, which by then wasn't even profitable, was all I had left in the world. I had to make it work or face losing everything."

"How on earth did you manage? You had all those operations on your hip and leg, and recuperation from each."

He chuckled bitterly. "There's nothing like work to speed your recovery. And I had plenty of that. About that time, an old college friend's mother, Betty Dunsmore, applied for a job as my bookkeeper. Seems her daughter had run off with some damned Arab and Betty needed a full-time job to keep her sanity. You met Betty a couple of weeks ago at Tina's party. Anyway, I needed someone I could trust. We worked well together and had some of the same motives. We both had lost daughters, in a way. Although they're alive somewhere in this world, they're now out of our lives. There isn't much either of us can do about our situations."

"You miss your little daughter, don't you?" Noelle propped herself up on her elbow and met his gaze closely.

He smiled and answered with a sigh. "My little Rosy! Ah, she's such a beauty. I'm sorry I don't know her better. She was born in Houston and was a month old before I even saw her. We never had a chance to go through those early years together. When she was about four years old we started spending an occasional day together. It was often disastrous and still is damn clumsy. I'm a stranger in her life. A stranger known as Daddy."

"Philippe, you'll just have to work harder at getting to know Rose. I'll help you."

His hand circled her bare waist and pulled her closer to his warmth. "Noelle, Noelle, you're so sweet and generous. You don't have to worry about me. You have your own problems."

"I care, Philippe. I care . . ." She wanted to add "I care very much," but didn't dare. This was a precious moment between them, and might be the perfect time. But something held her back. Noelle needed to know if it was deep caring for this man who held her so securely to his chest. Or was this intense attraction, this most intimate of physical acts the result of something stronger? Was it love she felt for Philippe?

Noelle, too, had waited too long for this night with Philippe. Although she didn't admit it, she had also dreamed of him. Imagined them together. Dreamed of making love with him. Noelle wrapped her arms around him, pressing her full breasts to the curly mass on his chest, and they fell asleep together.

However, for Noelle, sleep didn't last. Long before the Louisiana sun sent streaks of light above the magnificent magnolia outside her window, her dark eyes stared into the blackness. She lay quietly in Philippe's arms until she thought she would scream if she couldn't turn over. Trying desperately to keep her movements slight, she shifted, and he did too. She held her breath. Only one of them should have to suffer this wakefulness.

Philippe moved again and turned away from her, his broad, strong back uncovered, a muscular arm thrown around the pillow. Noelle's heart skipped a beat at the sight of him, so masculine and handsome. Her eyes traveled unavoidably down to the sheet, drawn tightly over his slim hips, and a painful twinge pierced her insides.

His scars, both physical and emotional, had been exposed to her tonight. They represented years of hell for Philippe. Knowing of his pain hurt her deeply, and endeared him to her more. It wasn't sympathy she felt for him; it was intense admiration. Philippe had overcome all odds to be where he was today. He was one of the strongest men she had ever known.

She sighed, remembering how open and off-handed he was about his disability. To hear him talk, it could have been a simple fractured arm or appendicitis. Just an accident, a fact of life, a wound. But it wasn't; it was a tragedy that left him lame for life, a tragedy that occurred in a war nobody cared about. *I care! Oh, I care, Philippe!* Her feelings surfaced in a swell of emotions that frightened her. This was not what she needed right now. Not this involvement, this . . . caring. *This love!* Philippe was right. She had to get her own life in order first before she could help him with his.

Making as little noise as possible, Noelle slid away from Philippe and the bed. She crossed to the window and gazed unseeingly at the large magnolia leaves that were barely outlined against a pale sky.

She thought about her feelings for Philippe. Certainly he thrilled her, as much—no, more than—he had in years past. But was it love? She honestly didn't want her already-complicated life cluttered with love right now. There was no room for a man. Even Philippe.

And yet, she couldn't imagine being without him. She had wanted him, needed him for so long, life would be empty without him. Especially now, after tonight. Their lovemaking had been a culmination of years of fantasizing and longing. And it had been grander than she ever dreamed.

Noelle realized, though, that life wasn't made of dreams. Now that she had played out her job fantasy, she had to face the harsh realities again. Being a street artist on Jackson Square had been fun and had fulfilled her desire to do what she had always wanted. However, she had to get back to teaching. It was all she knew; what she knew best. Teaching was what she wanted to do.

A sudden chill in the room sent a shiver down her back, and she hugged her arms closer in an attempt to warm her naked body.

"Noelle?" The masculine voice was tentative, and a large warm hand rested gently on her shoulder.

She turned into Philippe's welcoming arms, seeking his strength.

"Noelle, baby, are you all right?" His arms enclosed her protectively, hugging her close to his masculine warmth.

"Yes. No—I don't know what's wrong with me, Philippe. I just can't sleep."

"Is it because of us? Of what happened tonight? Does that disturb you, Noelle? Please, be honest with me."

"No, that's not it." She buried her face in his chest, reluctant to admit her love so soon. "I've . . . I've had this insomnia before. I guess I have too many things to worry about. Too much running through my mind."

"I wish I could help you, Noelle. What could be so bad that it keeps you awake nights?"

Noelle raised her head and looked honestly at him. Those tiger eyes were sincere and loving, and before she could stop herself, Noelle began to pour out her emotions. "Well, for one thing, I've got to have a job! Do you know how degrading it is to be unemployed? How frustrating? And I need a reasonable one. I can't live forever as a street artist. Not if I want to eat too. It was fun for a while, but it's not a permanent solution. I must teach, and yet, something deep inside me doesn't want to. I hate to admit it, but I really don't want to go back. I've failed so miserably. I'm scared to go back into the classroom. That's a terrible thing for a teacher to say! Scared!"

Sensibly, he said, "Then, don't go. Follow your instincts, Noelle."

"I have to go back! Teaching is all I've ever done. Anyway, I'm a good teacher. A damn good teacher! And I love it! I love the kids and—"

His hands gripped her shoulders, jostling her with his strength. "Noelle, Noelle, baby, take it easy. I love kids too. But, I'm not beating myself up to teach them. Maybe you need a break. There are other jobs—"

She shook her head stubbornly. "But it's different with me, Philippe. You just don't understand. I love teaching. I *am* a teacher. And I have to get back to it! Have to!"

Norm's words echoed in her mind. *It's like falling off a horse when you lose control. You have to climb right back on again.*

Philippe turned his head slightly, and evaluated her words, her torn emotions. "Noelle, you aren't making much sense. Think about it a minute. You want to teach, yet you don't. You must go back to the classroom, but you're scared. Now, which is it, baby?"

Sudden tears welled up in her eyes. He was right! She wasn't making sense! "I . . . don't know what I want, Philippe! I've never felt so bewildered in my life! I can't even make a decision anymore! I don't know what's—what's wrong with me!" The last words were squeezed out between sobs as she finally allowed her tortured feelings to surface in tears of agony.

Philippe's arms wrapped protectively around her and he lifted her slight form against his chest. Carrying her to the bed, he cuddled her like a child while she cried helplessly on his shoulder.

When she finally stopped sobbing Philippe spoke

gently. "I may be off-base, Noelle, but sounds to me like you're experiencing burnout. It happens sometimes, especially in a field like teaching, where you're constantly giving of yourself—"

Burnout? The words rose in her mind and Noelle rebelled against his theory with every fiber in her slight frame. She wanted to scream at him. It just couldn't be! Things like that didn't happen to good teachers!

"No! You're wrong! You don't know anything about me! You're dead wrong, Philippe Merritt!" Her words were vicious and spoken before she realized they were out.

Philippe retreated into silence, allowing her angry words to settle embarrassingly in the uneasy stillness that followed. He set her firmly on the bed and moved away from her.

In agony Noelle watched as he reached for his clothes and began pulling on his slacks. The light was pale and outlined his magnificent male form as he dressed without a word. Suddenly the acute realization of her angry words hit her. She had yelled at Philippe, insulted him. All he had done to elicit her wrath was to show his concern. What was wrong with her? She was driving away the only person who cared!

"Oh, Philippe, I'm sorry! I'm sorry!" She was beside him, her hand gripping his muscular arm, her dark eyes begging for forgiveness. "Don't . . . don't go. I didn't mean what I said. Please, don't go, Philippe . . . darling . . ."

112

He turned painful eyes her way, and their souls mingled in that one expressionless moment. The thread of emotion that pulled them together initially was miraculously taut again, and they were irrepressibly drawn into each other's arms. Seeking. Comforting. Caring. Binding an unacknowledged love that neither was willing to admit.

Their bodies molded together, muscular chest to bare, pliant breast; taut, rough skin to silky smoothness; masculinity to femininity. Their touching soothed away the rough edges of anger and unhappiness. Malicious words were forgotten as they made love again, this time slowly and leisurely. Philippe passionately explored every inch of her body. His kisses covered her, tasting and tempting until she clung to him, shamelessly begging for fulfillment.

Noelle returned the pleasure in every way she knew, wordlessly reassuring Philippe that his old injury didn't matter at all to her. Indeed, he was stronger and better for it.

In the frenzied moment of final union, his hands encircled her waist and he lifted her above his aroused form and settled her onto him, joining them in absolute splendor and beauty. They climbed the mountain in an unhurried, exquisite fashion. It was breathlessly glorious, and they exulted in their wondrous delight. They laughed and talked and encouraged each other. Together they were intrepid, invincible, and in love.

Wrapped in each other's arms, they slept until

noon. This time Noelle slept like a baby. She was secure and warm with Philippe.

They spent the weekend together, laughing and loving. It was almost like a honeymoon. Between the loving moments, they tried to catch up on everything during the past ten years. On Sunday night they parted reluctantly, their bodies satiated, their spirits refreshed.

Noelle was alone all week, since Philippe had business out of town. But it was just as well that she was alone. She had a job to find and a lot of thinking to do. She needed this time alone to ponder what had transpired between her and Philippe so quickly, so naturally. It seemed as though they had each endured the last ten years for this past glorious weekend together. Their coming together was so untamed, so mutually satisfying. Almost too perfect!

Noelle couldn't help but question her own emotions for this man whom she had loved from afar for so long. He seemed so willing to share, to love. But was she? Was she ready for love?

Tuesday morning Noelle showered and washed her hair, preparing for another job-hunt. She answered a knock on the door dressed in a turbaned towel and the audacious robe Philippe had disliked. She faced a woman who was almost as curiously dressed.

Clad in heavy lace-up boots, jeans, an impressive tool belt with all kinds of instruments dangling around her hips, the woman sported pink ribbons in her hair that matched her pink T-shirt. She was a combination of the ultimate in femininity and the fix-it man! It was all Noelle could do to keep from laughing aloud.

"You Noelle Clayton?" The woman read from a slip of paper attached to a clipboard, her words alternating between gum chews. The fruity fragrance was overpowering.

"Yes."

"I'm here to install your phone." She smacked her gum again and miraculously affixed the clipboard to yet another hook on the tool belt at her waist.

"Wait a minute," Noelle protested, adjusting the turban on her head. "I didn't order a telephone."

The woman's fist rested jauntily on her hip and she chewed a couple of times before responding. "Well, somebody did. It's for this address, St. Charles Street, Noelle Clayton. You gonna let me in?"

"I don't know what to do about this misunderstanding."

The woman shrugged. "You may as well take it. It's all paid for. Pretty phone too. Believe me, honey, if somebody ordered this fancy phone for me, I'd take it and wouldn't ask any questions!"

Philippe! It just had to be!

"Well, I—" Noelle stepped back, allowing the woman entry.

She headed instinctively for the bedroom, smacking her gum noisily. "Where do you want it? In your bedroom? It'll look real good in there."

Noelle stared at the telephone installer, a bewildered smile parting her lips. That damned, demanding, extravagant, lovable Philippe! This had to be his doing! He was the one perturbed over her not having a phone. He had fumed because he couldn't call her, fussed because she had no intention of getting one. Of course, he would do something about it, if he so chose. And apparently he did. How could she refuse?

She pointed out the location for the phone and proceeded to towel-dry her hair and dress for another day of job hunting. The sound of drilling reminded her that shortly she would have a fancy telephone installed in her bedroom, courtesy of Mr. Philippe Merritt!

Her first telephone call was from Philippe. "Hi, Noelle! God! Life away from you is dull! Get your glad rags ready, because I'll be in town Friday night, and we're going to every night spot in the *Vieux Carré!* It's time we celebrated New Orleans like it's supposed to be!"

"Philippe, about this phone?"

"Does it fit?" He laughed softly.

She held the exquisite brass and ivory instrument close to her smiling lips. "Yes," she whispered loudly. "It fits. But you shouldn't have."

His voice was low and sensuous. "I wanted to be able to talk to you. Wish I could be there this minute, baby, and make sure about the fitting myself. See you at seven Friday."

By the time Noelle answered his knock at the end

of the week, she wanted to fling herself into his arms and pour out her heart to him. It had been a frustratingly lonely week. Instead, she smiled happily, taking in his appearance. She knew this evening would be fun and full of laughter and maybe, for a little while, she could forget her joblessness.

"Hi. Miss me?" His tiger eyes searched her face for a reflection of the desire he felt for her.

"Yeah. Lots."

His hands took her shoulders, pulling her to him. "You look stunning."

"Thank you." She quivered before his inspection in her slinky black and white flapper-style dress with spaghetti straps and twelve-inch fringe that shimmered around her hips.

"I'll have to fight off the revelers on Bourbon Street tonight! That fringe drives me crazy!" Philippe teased as he brought her closer. "How are you?"

"Fine. But still unemployed."

"I don't care about that. Only about us. God, I've missed you this week!" His lips came down with such ferocity that she felt the pain of his teeth against her lips. He crushed her to him, lifting her off the floor in the process, molding her satin softness to his hard masculinity. There was no resisting his strength, no denying the physical demand of his hand cupping her buttocks, pressing her hips firmly to his.

He finally lifted his head with a low moan and kissed her neck all the way down to the exposed tops of her breasts. "Ah, Noelle . . . I want you. Now!"

Noelle clung to him tightly. "Philippe, hold me . . ."

His kisses traced her heated cleavage, seeking more than the satin dress would allow. She pressed achingly against his ardent mouth, desiring his touch with increasing intensity.

"Philippe," she murmured. "Would you like to see my new telephone? It's by the bed."

He swung her into his arms and smiled, those tiger eyes blazing with uncontrollable desire. "It's not the phone I want to see stretched out on your bed right now!"

She laughed delightedly, knowing that their celebration in the *Vieux Carré* tonight would have to wait.

CHAPTER SEVEN

Louie stood outside the closed bedroom door, switching his gray Persian tail angrily. His ears twitched as he listened to the sounds coming from inside. He paced the floor and eventually stalked through the living room. Springing to the sofa in one easy leap, Louie walked along the back of the sofa. He hunched there for a quick nap. It was a poor substitute for Noelle's bed.

However, right now, Noelle's bed was completely occupied, with no room for a jealous Persian cat!

Philippe's tanned, sandy-haired body lay sprawled halfway over Noelle's slick, slender form. His leg crossed both of hers, clamping her under him. But she lay comfortably nestled against his chest with no intention of moving. This moment was too wonderful to spoil.

On the floor, the fringe on Noelle's satin dress spread, fanlike, where it had been dropped. It was obvious that Philippe's neatly pressed slacks and shirt were discarded hurriedly. There was a casual disarray of masculine and feminine articles around the room. Ecru bikini panties here, navy blue briefs there.

Finally, from the two people spread-eagled on the bed, came a slight movement. A rumbled sound and a soft laugh were barely audible. The man's dark hand slid down to caress one exposed creamy breast, its cherry tip still pointed and hard from their lovemaking. He touched the circle of the swollen mound lovingly, then moved to the other.

"Philippe . . . oh, yes."

"Noelle, my beautiful Cajun baby." His hand did not stop its caressing. "They're so perfect. Did you know that?"

"What? I never noticed."

"I notice those kinds of things. Your breasts are lovely. And they're equal." He lowered his head to kiss each one.

She laughed a low, full sound. "Equal?"

"Sure. One is usually larger. Like feet. One foot is normally bigger. But not yours. They're perfect." His tongue taunted one peaked tip.

She was giggling. "How do you know? Have you measured? Maybe it's an optical illusion!"

"I'll count the kisses around each one. That should be a good gauge." He proceeded to kiss her into oblivion. When he finished circling each breast, he announced triumphantly, "Thirteen each! That's perfect to me!"

"Unlucky thirteen! Oh, Philippe," she laughed softly, tangling her fingers in his hair. "How did I ever manage before you came along to make me laugh again?"

"Lucky thirteen!" he amended. "Are you happy, Noelle?"

"With you I'm sublimely happy, Philippe. Can't you tell?"

"Is this the same lady who cried so miserably last weekend over some damned stupid job?"

"The same," she smiled sheepishly. "I want to apologize for that. I never should have aired my problems with you, Philippe. You have enough of your own."

"Don't apologize for being honest with me, Noelle. I knew from the beginning that something was bothering you. Thank God you trust me enough to discuss it. This is a situation we can handle. I was worried it might be another man. That's something I couldn't stand."

She slid her hands down to his shoulders and pulled him tightly to her, meshing the crisp masculine chest hair to her breasts. "There is no other man, Philippe."

"Well, I knew Nate was interested—"

"I told you, Philippe, Nate and I don't even fit," she teased with a grin.

He moved directly over her, molding her soft feminine shape beneath him in contrast to his hardness. "You mean, like this?"

Noelle could feel his arousal taunting her, and she

smiled devilishly. "We do fit perfectly, Philippe." She reached down and slid her hand between them, boldly adjusting their anatomy so the joining was inevitable.

"What an aggressive witch you are, my little Cajun baby!"

Her voice was a groan. "Ahhh, slow and easy this time, Philippe."

"Whatever you say, baby. I want to please you." He moved slowly, rhythmically. "Just for you . . . ah, Noelle, I love to see you respond to me. I love to make love to you!"

Leisurely, methodically, her body responded, moving in the ageless way of a woman's love for her man. With great restraint Philippe paced himself, postponing their culmination with disciplined skill. When Noelle began moving in a frenzy, arching against him with all her strength, he released his pent-up power to match her fervor. He thrust deeply into her, touching that spot of most sensitivity until her satisfying cry of ecstasy pierced the night.

All was quiet for a few minutes. Then, "Noelle, baby, are you all right?"

"Yes." She muffled, burying her face against his chest.

"Then, why are you crying?"

"I—I don't know. It's just so good, I can't help it." She wiped warm tears in Philippe's sandy chest hair.

"What? You aren't making any sense. Did I hurt you?" He turned her face up to his.

"No, of course not. Damn it, can't I cry without the third degree?"

"Not when I'm making love to you. I told you, I want you happy." He kissed her lips tenderly.

"I am, Philippe. Oh, I am."

Eventually they made it to the French Quarter. After a refreshing shower, and playfully dressing each other amid lots of laughter and teasing, they finally strode, arm in arm, down Bourbon Street. Dinner was a wonderful affair in the Rib Room of the Royal Orleans Hotel. They feasted on crusty bread spread with butter, and onion soup, thick with cheese. Then, like starved orphans, they shared oysters Rockefeller, a two-inch prime rib, and a bottle of palest fragrant Sauterne. Neither cared whether the wine was "correct" with their mixture of beef and seafood. They loved it, and just being together. That much was obvious.

After what seemed like hours, they moved on to Pat O'Brien's. In the spirit of the Quarter, they felt obliged to follow tradition and savor the famous house drink, the hurricane. Afterward, they were definitely cheered and felt in the mood for music. Philippe was mellow enough to suggest stopping by Preservation Hall for some New Orleans jazz. They sat for a few hours in the smoky room, enjoying the lively music almost as much as each other.

As they left the building Noelle smiled happily. "Thank you, Philippe. Listening to my favorite music shows your complete tolerance! And it was wonderful!"

"Glad you appreciate my sacrifice," he observed dryly. "Actually, the music was good tonight."

"Ah-ha! You're beginning to appreciate quality sounds!" she gloated.

"I'm admitting that if spending an evening with you entails listening to a few hours of Dixieland jazz, I'm game!" he amended, nuzzling her earlobe. "How would you like a little jaunt around the *Vieux Carré* in a horsedrawn carriage?"

She kissed his cheek. "Oh, I'd love it, Philippe! It's been years!"

Soon they were cloaked in each other's arms as a slow-gaited horse plodded around familiar buildings and parks throughout the French Quarter. Neither noticed, nor cared, where they were going. Noelle's eyes were closed in ecstasy and her lips were parted to receive Philippe's passionate kisses. His tongue sought her inner depths, gently teasing her lips open, plundering the sweet recesses of her mouth. She allowed his exploration, welcomed his intrusions, relished the masculine strength held at bay behind the kiss. Oh, God! She couldn't wait until they got home!

Noelle leaned against Philippe, delighting in the contact with his strong body. She wanted more than this public place would allow. She wanted to feel his flesh burning hers again, to know the reverberation of his pounding heart, to submit to his irresistible masculine power.

It was long, motionless minutes before either of them realized that the midnight ride was finished. They had traveled full circle around the Quarter, oblivious to the world. The carriage was still, with the patient driver and horse waiting for the lovers' passion to subside. Philippe scrambled to help Noelle from the carriage and pay the driver. Then they drove home in quiet contentment. It had been a lovely evening.

As they mounted the stairs to her apartment, she urged, "Please, come in."

"Are you sure?"

"Positive," she assured him. "I want you here with me all night."

He unlocked the door and swept her inside and into his arms. His kiss told her more than words ever could. Philippe's passion with her was once again strong, and Noelle anxiously awaited the silent promise of fulfilled desire. He lifted her in his powerful arms and carried her to the bed. With open arms Noelle accepted Philippe's love, hoping, secretly praying, it really was his love, not simply his desire that she was responding to. Yet neither was willing to admit love now. They knew only that everything was right between them, that they needed to be together. They shared laughter and joy. They were good for each other. Wasn't that enough for now?

"Tonight, *ma petite,* you will sleep. I promise . . ." Philippe buried a kiss between her perfect breasts, and Noelle arched against his touch, aching already for the satisfaction only Philippe could give her.

Morning came slowly into focus. Noelle basked lazily in the newness and wonder of Philippe's love. The nights left her blissfully exhausted, yet she awoke excitingly refreshed. She knew the physical completeness of satisfying lovemaking, as well as the security in having a companion who listened and laughed and cared just for her. She slept well for the first time in months.

It was perfect, this relationship with Philippe. Or was it? They couldn't go on forever living this way, satisfying their physical needs on weekends. She found herself thinking about him all the time and wanted him near. She cared much too much for him, she realized, to ever be satisfied with a casual affair.

A muscular, hairy leg crossed hers. "Noelle? You awake?"

"Hmmm," she sighed tranquilly, reaching out a hand to rest on his taut skin. She spread her fingers to encompass and caress the rounded buttock, mentally noting that this wasn't the hip with the scar. Most of the time, she forgot about his injury. It had become something that didn't matter at all to her. She was beginning to understand Philippe's casual attitude about it.

His hand wandered from her waist to her bare breast, toying with the relaxed nipple. "I have a confession. I have never been so satisfied in my life. You're amazing, for a little snip of a girl."

She smiled and opened one eye. "Well, I have never been so loved in my life! You're inexhaustible!"

"Thank you." His laughter rumbled. "It's a good thing we agree on something." He turned and cradled her in his arms.

Noelle nuzzled his neck, kissing and teasing his skin with her tongue. "I agree . . ."

In the beautiful quiet that followed, they could hear Louie's plaintive meowing outside the closed bedroom door.

"I wish we could stay here all day. However, Louie will probably be delighted that I have a previous commitment. I've taken your advice, Noelle. I'm bringing my little Rosy to New Orleans, after considerable discussion with her mother. I'll be picking her up at the airport later this morning." Philippe caressed Noelle's arm lovingly.

"Wonderful, Philippe! But why didn't Marion want her to come?" Noelle shivered slightly at his touch and snuggled closer under his arm. It was heaven to lie, relaxed, in Philippe's arms. She wished they could stay this way all day. Everything was perfect between them. The only thing that marred her life right now was the fact that she still hadn't found a job.

"Oh, I guess Marion's just being a typical mother, not wanting to lose control of her child. But she finally relented." He shrugged.

"Maybe Marion's control is what sways Rose's attitude when she spends time with you in Houston. Children are deeply influenced by the adults closest to them. I think you'll have a good time with Rose here in New Orleans. At least, you'll have an even chance. You know, of course, that not every moment a parent spends with his or her child is terrific. So, don't expect too much either."

He sighed. "Ah, but we have such a short time together, every moment is precious. And I guess I want it to be perfect. You have such insight into children, I appreciate your help and opinions, Noelle."

She shrugged and grinned. "Sure, any time my opinion is requested, I'll be glad to spout it. Sometimes even when it isn't!"

"Noelle, you have more experience with kids than I do. Would you consider going with us today? It would help me feel more at ease. We're going to take in the usual tourist things: the zoo, a paddleboat ride on the Mississippi, the French Quarter. These are all things she's never done. Why don't you come with us?"

Noelle smiled, but shook her head. "Thanks, but you need to be alone with your daughter. It wouldn't do much for your relationship with her if you dragged me along."

"It might be better," he countered.

"You aren't afraid to be alone with your daughter, are you?" Noelle tweaked his nose teasingly. "She's just a little girl."

128

"It's the little ones that I can't handle!"

"But, the big ones—" Noelle reared threateningly close, hands on her bare hips.

He laughed mischievously. "The big ones I can handle, but they have me completely baffled too! I don't claim to understand them at all!"

"You eased out of that one, Mr. Merritt. Tell you what. You spend the day with Rose, doing whatever the two of you want to do. And remember, you don't have to occupy every minute of the day. Sometimes doing nothing can be fun. You have quite a day planned, and little girls get tired, you know. Then, tonight, you can bring her here for a party. Tina's family is coming over for a little family celebration with Aunt Donda and me. We're going to do the cooking!" Noelle smiled grandly.

"You and Aunt Donda?"

"Yep. She's such a dear. And she has been so encouraging and sweet these last couple of weeks. She thinks teachers are perfect people, and I don't want to ruin her image!"

"Shall I have a talk with the lady to clear up any misconceptions?" he laughed.

"You—" Noelle pointed her finger accusingly "—stay away from her! I like it when someone recognizes my true talents!"

"Oh, I recognize your true talents, my little Cajun baby!" He nuzzled her neck. "I don't know about teaching, but you sure learn fast!"

"Now, now, Philippe. We both have things to do! You have to pick your daughter up at the airport.

And I'm taking Aunt Donda shopping! She knows all the special markets, and we're going to buy the best ingredients for okra gumbo and jambalaya and shrimp creole! Do you think Rose will like our food?" Noelle rolled out of the bed and began to gather the clothes that lay scattered on the floor.

"If Rose doesn't like it, we can get her a Big Mac. Cajun food sounds fabulous to me! I haven't had real gumbo in years. First, you have to start with a good roux. That's what all the good French cooks say."

Noelle scoffed at his advice. "What would you know about a good roux?"

"I know it's made with flour and oil, cooked for a long time in a skillet."

"Drippings and spices," Noelle amended, then slipped into panties as she continued. "I'm sure Rose will like the fry bread with honey." She pulled on jeans and a T-shirt, then, with a vengeful laugh, flipped the covers off Philippe's naked body. "Get up, you lazy bum! Your daughter will be waiting for you and Aunt Donda for me!"

Louie made himself heard again. The meowing had evolved into an angry growl.

"You little black-eyed witch! You and your damned wicked cat are conspiring against me!" In a flash Philippe had encircled her with his arms and was kissing her unmercifully all over.

Noelle struggled, laughing. "I didn't know you could move so fast!"

"Ah, *ma chérie,* there's so much about me that you don't know!"

She stopped struggling and placed her arms lovingly around his neck. "But, I'm loving the learning. Philippe, oh, Philippe . . ." The last words were a soft whisper.

"Ah, my little Cajun baby, me too . . ." His kiss quieted them both and sent them spiraling together in the path of love and passion. Finally, with difficulty, Noelle persuaded Philippe to relinquish his hold on her, knowing the busy day ahead didn't permit them the languid lovemaking she so fervently desired.

As the humid Louisiana evening settled over the huge magnolia tree and moss-draped oak, strains of laughter rose above the sweet fiddle music and the little bricked patio. A small but lively Cajun party was just beginning. It was hard to tell whose spirits were higher, Noelle's or Aunt Donda's! However, a special glow lit Noelle's eyes when someone called, "Here comes Philippe!"

They turned to see Philippe hauling a huge galvanized tub. A beautiful golden-haired, large-eyed child followed him closely, an apprehensive expression on her face. The only resemblance between father and daughter were the brown-flecked tiger eyes.

"At last, Philippe!" Aunt Donda greeted him with a sly smile and pointed to a low table. "Set the tub over here."

Philippe settled his burden and turned first to the elderly woman. He kissed her on both cheeks and smiled proudly. "This is my daughter, Rose." Bringing the child forward, he urged, "Rose, this is Aunt Donda."

Rose smiled bashfully and recited in a sweet Texas accent, "Pleased to meet you, Aunt Donda." She offered the woman a small bouquet of six yellow roses.

"Why, thank you, Rose. They're beautiful!" Aunt Donda smiled gratefully, taking the flowers in her fragile hand. "What a beautiful child, Philippe. And so polite."

Philippe swallowed a nervous smile. "Thank you, Aunt Donda." Then he turned Rose toward the others who gazed curiously at the lovely child before them. "This is Noelle. Her sister, Tina. And this is Tina's husband, Max. And their daughter, Brianna." Rose shook hands all around, but her brown eyes smiled with promise when she caught sight of Brianna.

Brianna, who was suddenly the "older girl," took Rose's hand. "Noelle has a cat upstairs. Do you want to go see him?"

"Can I, Daddy?" Rose asked courteously.

"Sure, sweetheart." Philippe nodded.

The two girls headed up the side stairs to Noelle's apartment, and Philippe breathed an obvious sigh of relief.

"She's a darling child, Philippe." Tina smiled graciously. "Now, what have you brought?" She walked over to the tub which was filled with ice.

Philippe grinned devilishly, winking at Aunt Donda. He reached down into the icy tub. "Something special for all of you from Rose and me!" he announced, pulling out a large, ruffled oyster shell.

"Ohhh!" The sound was a mutual exclamation, blending the adults' voices into one.

"And you must have them the natural way, New Orleans style!" He accepted the large knife Aunt Donda handed him and, with one twist of his strong arm, popped the oyster open.

"The natural way? What's that?" Noelle questioned, her dark eyes large and curious.

Philippe's eyes traveled for a brief, wicked glance at Aunt Donda, then back to Noelle. "This is the very best way to enjoy oysters, Noelle. And, since you've been away from New Orleans so long, I want you to be the first to savor this delicacy." He held the open oyster shell out to her and instructed, "Just put your lips on it and pucker like you were going to give it a big kiss. Then, suck it up! The natural way!"

Noelle gave him a horrified look. "You're out of your mind. I couldn't—"

"Back in my day, we ate them that way all the time!" Aunt Donda offered testily. "Here, I'll show you!"

Before the others could blink, the elderly lady slipped the curly oyster through her lips and swallowed with a satisfied grin. "Now, where's my beer?"

"You aren't going to let Aunt Donda get the best of you, are you, Noelle?" Philippe taunted, reaching for another oyster.

Through thin, stubborn lips, she muttered, "I can do it." She glanced pleadingly at Max. "Have my drink ready!" Noelle put her lips on the cold, salty oyster. Squeezing her eyes shut, she sucked. For a brief, panicky moment, she feared the thing wouldn't go down, or, worse yet, would come back up! Then, miraculously, the oyster slipped down her throat, and she grabbed for the beer Max held!

Everyone applauded and cheered encouragingly. The precedent was set, though, and everyone had to experience oysters "the natural way" at least once! "The natural way" was inevitably followed by half a beer, gulped nonstop! Later, Aunt Donda graciously prepared a spicy piquante sauce for the remainder of the raw appetizers.

"Philippe, you're a devil for bringing those things," Noelle complained.

He arched his eyebrows. "It was Aunt Donda's idea! She's a 'real dear,' remember? So sweet and—"

"So you two contrived this little deal?" She eyed the petite lady who was waltzing with Max.

He shrugged innocently. "We felt that we had to break the ice somehow."

"Speaking of breaking the ice, Brianna seems to have done just that with Rose."

"Thank God for Brianna! If she hadn't been here, we would really have trouble!"

"Why, Philippe, I can't believe that. Rose is a lovely, sweet child."

He rolled his eyes and held his head in agony. "Lovely, yes. But, sweet? Ha! The perfect child she isn't! I almost called you for advice an hour ago."

"Advice? Why? Didn't you two have a good time today?"

"Oh, yes, Noelle. We had a wonderful time together, just the two of us. But, you were right. I had too much planned. We'll have to take a ride on the Mississippi another time. I showed her where I work, then we went to the zoo. Later, we went home, relaxed, and swam awhile. That was the trouble. She didn't want to leave the pool. She had no interest in coming over here with a bunch of strangers—and adults, to boot. She threw a goddamn screaming fit!" He shook his head. "I just couldn't deal with it."

"That darling little angel?" Noelle teased, knowing full well how changeable kids could be. "What did you do? She seemed so willing tonight, giving roses to Aunt Donda and generally being the most polite child I've ever seen."

He grinned. "Well, there was a little bribery involved. Actually, a threat was more like it. I told her if she didn't shut up, I would send her back home to her mother. Tonight!"

"Philippe! You wouldn't do that!" Noelle said.

"No, but she doesn't know it!"

"Oh, you're fast learning some of the tricks of parenthood!" Noelle conceded with a laugh.

They joined Tina in the white wrought-iron chairs that circled the brick patio, and watched as Max whirled a spry Aunt Donda to another waltz.

"Philippe, these oysters are terrific. They're very sweet and mild," Tina commented dryly. "But, I must admit I prefer them with piquante sauce."

He grinned devilishly. "Why, I can't imagine why you don't want them 'the natural way,' Tina!" He reached into the icy tub and popped several oyster shells, leaving them open and on ice for anyone who wanted to partake.

"Well, I can!" Noelle sniffed. "I've lived here almost all my life and have never heard of oysters 'the natural way!' I think it's something you invented, Philippe Merritt!"

"Just because you don't travel in the correct Cajun circles doesn't mean others don't enjoy the finest!" With typical flair, Philippe popped another raw oyster into his mouth.

"Ooooh!" Both Noelle and Tina made faces as they remembered the briny taste.

Philippe had great fun teasing them all evening, and when the girls finally returned from their visit with Louie, he offered them a nice fat oyster.

With childish squeals of protest, they scattered.

Max was kept busy throughout the night, dancing with the women, plus the two bashful little girls. It was a wonderfully casual, family-oriented evening, and everyone enjoyed themselves. They ate okra gumbo and shrimp jambalaya and crawfish étouffée until they could eat no more. They danced until Max finally stumbled, hot and out of breath, onto the elegantly laced wrought-iron love seat, begging for rest.

"Come on, Daddy. Why don't you ever dance with me?" Rose entreated, tugging persuasively on Philippe's hand.

Philippe shook his head uncomfortably. "Oh, Uncle Max moves so much smoother than I. Anyway, I don't know how to waltz."

"I'll show you how, Daddy," Rose implored. "It isn't hard. Uncle Max taught me. You just count one, two, three, together!"

"Not tonight, darling." Philippe's face hardened with embarrassment.

"Please," begged his daughter. Obviously, no one ever refused her requests.

"No, Rose! And that's final! Leave me alone!"

The little girl's large brown eyes rose to meet her father's. "I wish you were like other daddies who do fun things." She turned and walked away, embarrassment and hurt showing on her small face.

Philippe stuffed his hands into his pockets and strode alone across the patio.

Noelle started to follow him, but halted. Something told her he needed to be alone. It was the first time Noelle had ever seen him so obviously embarrassed by whatever inconvenience his injured leg caused. He was usually so frank and honest about his condition. Why didn't he just explain it to Rose?

Max took her hand. "It's best to ignore this, Noelle. He has to work this out himself. How about a dance? This one's a slow one. I think I can manage. Looks like I opened a can of worms with this dancing business."

Noelle fell into step with him. "No, Max. It's not your fault. Like you said, Philippe has to learn to handle this, and other problems, with his daughter."

Later, as Philippe and Rose prepared to leave, he turned to Noelle. "Rose and I are going to Rosewood tomorrow. Will you go with us? Please." There was a plaintive tone to his request.

"Oh, yes, please go, Noelle," Rose squealed. "And can Brianna come along too?" She clutched her father's hand. Could it be that she wanted to patch things up between them, in her childish way?

"Rosewood?" Noelle wrinkled her brow. The Merritt family plantation held old memories, and she wasn't sure if she wanted to revive them yet.

Philippe turned to Max and Tina. "How about it? Could Brianna go along too? We'd love to have her."

Tina shrugged. "If she would like to go, it's fine with me."

Brianna nodded enthusiastically. "Oh, yes! I'd love it! Are you going, Aunt Noelle?"

She smiled at the two girls. "Sure. Why not?"

Soon it was settled. Noelle and Philippe would take the girls for a picnic to the old plantation the next day.

Philippe took Noelle's hand and kissed it. "Until

tomorrow then." His eyes promised more, but, Noelle knew that night she would sleep alone.

"Why don't you kiss her, Philippe?" Brianna taunted with a sly gleam in her youthful eyes. She grinned at Rose, who stared curiously at Brianna, then her father.

Philippe leaned forward and kissed Noelle's lips lightly, and everyone cheered. Then they were gone, leaving Noelle with a sweet, soft kiss that would linger in her mind all through the night.

CHAPTER EIGHT

Philippe's hands gripped the steering wheel, and he looked down at his legs. With bitterness his eyes traveled over the injured one. He knew its inadequacy, its disability, and had thought he had long since come to terms with it. But at that moment a deep rage welled up inside him at his own limitations.

Years ago Philippe decided to overcome this injury, to live with it, to beat it completely. He wasn't even bitter when Marion left. She just couldn't handle all the problems that confronted them. That was life. Anyway, their love had fled before her, so the parting wasn't devastating.

But having a child he didn't know was increasingly frustrating. How could he show his love for Rose when they lived apart? Why couldn't he explain his struggles to achieve, the difficulties he had overcome? Why couldn't he tell his daughter how he had accomplished all this? Would this stranger who called him Daddy understand?

Somehow, he couldn't bring himself to tell his young daughter the real truth. He couldn't let her know that he was inadequate in some way. It was ridiculous! His ego was at stake here. He could handle adults, but was stymied by a child. However, this was *his* child, and he wanted desperately to be her hero. To be everything she needed. To be like "other daddies." But he wasn't. He could accept it for himself. Even for Noelle. He just couldn't admit it to his daughter. *Damn it! How kids twist you up inside!*

He glanced at Noelle. She was so lovely, so understanding. She relaxed with her head lolled back on the headrest, her dark hair fanned on the burgundy seat cover. God, he longed to dig into that hair, to explain his feelings to her, to feel her close to him, to know that she cared for him, no matter what.

Noelle smiled at him. "Oh, Philippe, it's so beautiful here. I've missed these moss-draped trees and this—this gorgeous land!" Her face glowed with delight as they rode deeper into the lush vegetation and fan-trails of creeks and rivers that meshed with the land.

"Beautiful? Aunt Noelle! Really!" Brianna sighed dramatically from the backseat where she kept company with little Rose, but listened to the adults in the front seat of Philippe's Mercedes.

"Someone once said that this place couldn't make

up its mind whether it would be earth or water, so it compromised," Philippe commented as he drove them over bridge after bridge.

"Looks like the water won." Noelle laughed.

"What do you think of all this, Rose?" Philippe prompted his small daughter to contribute to the conversation.

Her brown-flecked eyes danced with childish excitement. "This looks like a jungle to me. It's scary."

He caught her glance in the rearview mirror and teased with an exaggerated warning, "Are you watching for those 'gators?"

"Oh, Daddy!" she smiled apprehensively, not wanting to believe him, yet not sure. "There aren't any alligators out there!"

"Sure there are! Watch carefully, and I'm sure you'll see one. He looks like an old dead log. Only, he has eyes—watching you watch him!"

"Ohhh, Daddy!" Rose giggled, then quietly pressed her nose to the back window to watch warily.

Noelle smiled contentedly as the Louisiana countryside flashed past. Oaks and willows and cypresses formed arched shadows on the motionless water that curled lazily on either side of the highway. The car rolled rapidly into a land that appeared to have lost track of time. Even that was somehow comforting to Noelle though.

This trip was a good idea. It had started out happily with the girls eager and in good spirits. Even

Philippe seemed more relaxed than usual, especially when it came to dealing with Rose. Noelle was convinced he could manage his problems with her. He handled everything else so well. A youthful voice piped from the backseat, interrupting her thoughts.

"Oooh, look at all the pretty flowers! What kind are they, Daddy?"

Anyone in the car could have answered the question, but Rose sought the response from her father. Obviously she needed his answers to her never-ending questions.

Philippe motioned to the almost-solid layer of lavender orchidlike flowers blanketing the pond. "Those are water hyacinths. They grow on ponds or bayous, choking out all other growth."

"Hyacinths? Do they float?"

"Well, not exactly. Their roots go down into the water, while the flowers and leaves grow above it, cutting off oxygen and light for the other plants and animals that live there."

"Hyacinths stop photosynthesis!" Brianna announced triumphantly and sat back, beaming with pride at having used so adult a word.

"You're exactly right, Brianna," Philippe nodded. "The water hyacinth isn't native to Louisiana. It was brought here as a part of a Japanese exhibit nearly a hundred years ago. Each visitor received a flower as a souvenir. Little did anyone realize the problems these pretty little flowers would cause in bayou country. Over the years, even the Army

Corps of Engineers has been called in to try to eliminate the things. But still they survive."

"Hardy little devils, aren't they?" Noelle observed dryly, then grinned at Philippe. "My, you're full of information today."

He cast her a disparaging glance. "I'm in my fatherly role today."

"And you're doing a very fine job of it too." She smiled teasingly.

"Then pipe down and let me do my thing."

"Oh, I can't help teasing you, Philippe. You're so . . . so earnest about all this."

He pressed his lips together, thinking she was right. He was damned serious about this "fatherly" business. Maybe too serious for his own good. Finally they turned onto a narrow, paved road. The land was flat, but covered with lush vegetation. Philippe announced tightly, "Here we are, girls. This is Rosewood."

They emerged from the narrow road to view a typical old-South mansion of eighteenth-century vintage. A lane parted two rows of magnificent live oaks, leading directly to the front door of the antebellum house. As they drove down that lane, the branches of the oaks formed a shaded archway that covered them completely, ushering them back in time. They could have been traveling in a horse-drawn carriage a hundred years ago.

When they reached the house, Noelle could see its disrepair. Years of neglect and exposure to the harsh southern Louisiana weather had taken their toll. Shutters hung precariously from rusty hinges and paint scaled from the once-white frame building.

"This is where you lived when you were a little boy, Daddy?"

"Yep."

"What was it like in the olden days? Did you have TV?"

"Olden days? Why, you little snippet! I'm not that old! Of course, we had TV!"

"Did you play here?"

"Sure. Jumped off the porch over there. Climbed that tree. Hey, come on gang! Let's get out!"

His words were a signal that broke the magic woven by the moss-draped trees and ancient house. Everyone tumbled out of the confines of the Mercedes, and Philippe spent the next hour showing them around. They toured every empty, echoing room where windows were still hung with heavy velvet curtains. They walked the main property, careful to stay on the bricked pathways.

As they started back toward the house, Rose asked, "Daddy, can Brianna and I stay and play here in this old garden?"

"Sure. But be careful," he warned. "Stay on the path and away from the barns and thick undergrowth. They're unsafe. Don't play long. Lunch will be ready soon."

Brianna nodded seriously. "We'll be careful, Uncle Philippe."

He smiled at the girls, then turned to Noelle.

145

"Noelle and I will be waiting on the porch." His arm curved around her shoulders as they walked down the path. "By all appearances, Rose is the perfect child. Beautiful and well-behaved. But I know better," he chuckled derisively.

"Philippe, you must understand that no child is perfect. She is a little person who is having to adjust to her life, just like all the rest of us."

"She's moody, like her mother. And temperamental. And, I'll admit, spoiled. Perhaps what she needs is a daddy to be with her more often."

"I'd say that's a pretty good assessment," Noelle agreed gently.

"Noelle, I want to thank you for insisting that I bring her here. She has been much easier to handle this weekend. Maybe it's because she knows her mother isn't a phone call away, like she is in Houston. The most important reason, of course, is that we've had some very good times just being together.

"Plus, I'm finding out things about . . . about both of us."

"Oh? Like what?"

"Well, for one thing, little girls ask a lot of questions!"

Noelle laughed. "That, too, is pretty normal for kids her age. She's okay, Philippe. Actually, I'm glad you invited me and Brianna today. Rosewood was so beautiful in its day. It's sad to see it go to ruin."

They climbed the steps that led up to the porch and sat on the top one before he spoke. "I know. We still farm the rice fields to the south, but that's such a small part of my operation I don't even oversee it anymore. I just can't afford the time to be out here. I keep the house purely for sentimental reasons. I wanted Rose to see this part of her heritage."

"I think she'll remember this day for a long time. It's obvious Rosewood was once a very beautiful plantation. There are a lot of memories for you here, aren't there, Philippe?"

He nodded. "I remember one particular hurricane when I was a kid. The water came up to the second floor stairs! It ruined everything on the first floor. We cleaned out mud and debris for weeks afterward. God, what a mess!"

Noelle shook her head. "Rosewood feels so peaceful and tranquil now, it's hard to imagine a storm ravaging through here, doing that kind of damage." She watched a breeze catch the Spanish moss and wave it gently from the oak branches.

"I can still hear that wind whine through the windows! It can be vicious and frightening, especially when you're young. I remember a poem we used to recite during storms when we were scared. 'Over their heads the towering and tenebrous boughs of the cypress/ Met in a dusky arch, and trailing mosses in mid-air/ Waved like banners that hang on the walls of ancient cathedrals.' "

"Philippe, that's from Longfellow's *Evangeline*. What a romantic you are! How beautiful!"

"Romantic!" he scoffed, now somewhat abashed by what he had done. "My fourth grade English teacher made us memorize and recite great passages from *Evangeline* and it's wedged in my brain forever! It was a part of our history, she claimed. I'll never forget her."

"Or the things she taught you."

He looked at her curiously. "Is that the kind of teacher you are, Noelle?"

"I don't know," she answered reflectively. "But I suppose that's one of the reasons I love to teach. To feel I've played an important part in shaping a young person's life."

He nodded. "That's not a bad reason."

"Suddenly you make it sound a little selfish or self-centered. Doing good for others for the benefits I receive."

"Oh, no, Noelle. I think it's perfectly natural. We all want to be able to influence others in a positive way. You teachers just seem to have more of that drive than the rest of us."

"The urge to give of yourself . . ."

"It's also quite common for someone like you, who has taught for a number of years, to experience burnout. Many people in helping professions reach a point where they can't give of themselves anymore."

Noelle stiffened. "I don't feel that way. I love teaching."

"Sweetheart, it's okay to admit you've reached your limits. It just means that things got to be too much for you. We all have those times."

"But I haven't!" She was getting annoyed at his attitude.

"Noelle, you're showing many of the signs. Insomnia, running from the problem by changing from one job to another, inability to make a decision, even your attempt to be a street artist points to your job-related problems."

"I don't have job-related problems!" she protested stoutly. "What do you mean, 'showing all the signs'? You sound like a goddamn textbook!"

"I've been doing some reading, Noelle. I'm concerned about you."

She stood up. "Been reading up on me, huh? Well, you can damn well stop trying to be a textbook psychiatrist! I can take care of myself! I did before you came back into my life, Philippe Merritt, and I can now! Just stop interfering! I want to teach, and you're trying to talk me out of it! Some friend!"

"I'm not trying to talk you out of it. I'm saying that you're tired. You've given of yourself until there isn't any more to give. But there are other things you can do, if you'll calm down and just think about it. Let's discuss it!"

"Damn it, Philippe! There isn't anything to discuss! You don't understand me at all! If I wanted to do something else, I'd have taken the job Nate offered!"

"What job?" Philippe's eyes cut into her, and the old jealousy hovered in his mind.

Noelle raised her chin. "He offered to get me a

job at the station where he works. I might just take him up on it! Is that what you want?"

"Well, go right ahead! Work with that giraffe if you want to. Hell, if I thought you wanted to work somewhere else, I'd give you something at my company!"

"Damn it, Philippe! I don't want to do anything else! I don't want to work with Nate or you! I want to teach. If you understood me, you'd know that!"

He grabbed her shoulders. "I understand you all too well. I see a different person before me from the Noelle I loved. Yes, *loved!* I see someone who is erratic. Who can't sleep. Someone who has lost the fun of life and the old sense of humor because you're so damned busy giving! Giving of yourself to shape someone else's life while yours falls apart! And you don't have sense enough to see it!"

"It's my life! How dare you tell me I don't have sense—"

Their argument was pierced by the shattering scream of a child. Philippe was instantly moving in the direction of the sound, his voice loud and hoarse. "Rose! Rose!"

Noelle followed him, wondering wildly how he could move so fast with his limp. Visions of snakes and alligators filled her with fear. This low country could be dangerous.

"The sound came from the creek!" Philippe shouted ahead of her.

Noelle raced after him, breathless, her heart pounding. They rounded a turn and spotted Rose

150

sprawled on her stomach. Brianna bent over her, talking, calling her name. Panicky screams continued to pierce the air.

"Rose? Rosy, baby, what's wrong?" Philippe was beside her, lifting her into his strong arms.

"Daddy! Daddy, I fell!" She sobbed and began to brush her stomach and legs.

"Are you all right?" His voice was stern, his question a demand.

Rose curled her arms around her father's neck. "Yes, Daddy. But, I saw . . . I saw something horrible on the ground. What is that thing? I thought it was going to get me."

They looked in the direction her chubby finger pointed. There, in the moist earth under ferns and spiderworts, was a curious coral-colored plant. A closer look revealed that it was a sundew, a carnivorous plant, and a tiny spider was caught in its sticky tentacles. When Rose fell she had been nose to nose with the vigorous plant and struggling, captured spider.

Philippe was furious. "You scared the hell out of us, Rose! There's no need for this incessant screaming! And that"—he gestured with his thumb—"is just a plant that happens to eat bugs!"

"But it scared me. I thought it was going to get me!" she pouted.

"That's ridiculous! It's just a little sundew!"

"Philippe," Noelle interrupted gently. "If Rose is okay, why don't we have our picnic? Do you like fried chicken, Rose?"

"Yes, ma'am," the child nodded and took Noelle's outstretched hand. They retreated to the picnic, but everyone was subdued. After the brief argument between Philippe and Noelle and the scare from Rose, there wasn't much to say. They ate quietly, then returned to New Orleans. The family day was over, and Rose had to be boarded on a flight to Houston.

Noelle knew that she and Philippe had reached an impasse. Their argument had demonstrated how little he knew about her. Or cared. It was an upsetting realization. There was only one person who would understand. Tina.

"I don't know what to say. Of course, it's possible, Noelle."

"But it's not true, Tina! I'm not burned out. I love teaching."

"I know you do, Noelle. And there's no reason you can't continue teaching. We just need to find you a job. And that'll happen soon, I'm sure. Did you leave your resume with the state organization as Max suggested?"

"Yes," Noelle nodded, fiddling with her glass of tea. They sat on Tina's screened porch amid numerous green plants, overlooking the garden patio. The huge oak provided shade and a gentle breeze rustled through the leaves. "I think Philippe just doesn't understand me. And, obviously, he isn't even trying. He just sees things his way."

"And you want him to know how you feel. Did you tell him?"

"Of course. At least, I tried. But he kept talking about 'the signs' and how tired I was. Tired! How could I be? Why, I haven't worked in weeks, unless you count that one week down at Jackson Square. He just doesn't care about how I feel."

"I think he cares very much, Noelle," Tina smiled. "And you, my dear baby sister, have the look of a woman in love."

"In love with Philippe? Oh, no! We're just—just good friends. After all, we go back a long way."

"And the flame is still glowing, Noelle."

Noelle shook her head vehemently. "No, Tina. We're too different. And, he's too . . . Well, he's just not right for me. I've failed once, and I intend to make sure the next time it's perfect."

"Perfect!" scoffed Tina. "There's no such thing!"

"Oh, yes, there is. I'm holding out for someone like Max. He's an excellent father and provider. He's fun. He can dance like a dream. And he loves you!" Noelle laughed. "What more would I want!"

Tina wasn't amused and gazed wistfully over the patio. Her tone was subdued. "Yes, he loves us. But Max is far from perfect. He—" She stopped suddenly.

"What is it, Tina?" Noelle sensed deep feelings of bitterness in her sister. "Oh, I'm sorry. I don't want to pry."

But Tina continued. "Oh, Max is wonderful. If only he could keep us out of debt. He just took out another loan last week. He thinks he needs a new car."

"Tina, please, don't—"

Tina turned flashing eyes toward her sister. "Don't what? Don't tell you his faults? Don't tell you he runs us deeper in debt each year? Don't ruin your illusion of my 'perfect' husband?"

Noelle stood and turned away, breathing deeply. This was not at all what she expected from her sister. Nor was it what she wanted to hear. "Tina, don't tell me these things. They're private. I—I don't want to hear them."

"I'll bet you don't! You don't want to hear that everything we have here is covered by loans. That nothing is paid for—nothing! That if he has a dollar in his pocket, he spends two. That money sifts through his fingers like sand through a sieve! That I have to work in order to keep up the payments. When I get one bill paid off, he has two more for us."

Noelle turned around to see large tears swell in Tina's eyes. "But, Tina, he offered to loan me money until I get on my feet."

"And he meant it too. He would go out and borrow the money to loan you, so you wouldn't know he didn't have it. He's very generous and loving and wants to give us everything, even if it's more than he has!"

"I just can't believe it. How can you live like that?"

"There are times when I can't stand it. I have to

watch our finances very closely. And I'm the one who worries about paying off the loans. He doesn't."

Noelle placed her hand on Tina's shoulder. "It just doesn't sound like the Max I know. I'm sorry, Tina."

Tina shook her head and took a long drink of tea. "I probably shouldn't have told you all that. You just got me started when you said he was perfect. He isn't. But he loves us. And I'm not going to divorce him because he can't manage money worth a damn. After all, I love him."

"Yes, I can see you do." Noelle took one last sip of her tea, then set it on the beautiful glass and wrought iron table. She wondered briefly if the table, too, was still being paid for. Then she realized that it didn't matter. This was none of her business, and she should never have learned about it. She wished she didn't. She wished she didn't know a lot of things.

"Maybe you could teach Max about money management," Noelle offered weakly.

"Maybe I could work a miracle and change him after twelve years of marriage!" Tina scoffed.

"If you figure out how to do that, let me know, will you?"

Tina smiled and put a gentle hand on Noelle's shoulder. "I guess what I'm saying is that nobody's perfect. If you love Philippe, don't let him slip away. He's a remarkable person."

"I know it. Maybe understanding will come in

time." She stood up. "Good luck with your miracles, Tina. I've got to go. I'll talk to you later this week. Maybe I'll work a miracle of my own and produce a job!"

Tina stood and hugged her younger sister. "I hope so! Hey, I'm sorry for unloading on you like that. I shouldn't have. I know you'll keep it private between us two."

"Of course . . ."

"Noelle, I'm afraid you're looking for such perfection in your life, you're overlooking the important things. Perfection is an illusion, whether it's in a job or in a man you love. It's just a dream. Love is what really matters."

"Just a dream?" Noelle repeated gently. "You're beginning to sound like an old philosopher, Tina."

"No," Tina smiled in return. "Just an older sister who cares about you. I want you to find happiness."

"I'm looking, Tina. You're right. I'm still looking for that perfect dream."

Tina smiled warmly and watched Noelle walk across the garden patio and climb into her battered green VW. She bit her lips nervously, wondering if she had said too much and worrying that Noelle would throw away what was really important in her life. But that would have to be her decision.

Noelle shifted gears and wove in and out of traffic down St. Charles Street. It was a lovely area, her favorite part of town, but still her mind wandered wildly. She thought of Tina's confession, still shocked to learn of Max and Tina's financial problems. It shattered several of her illusions.

She remembered Philippe and his ability to make her feel like she could conquer the world. Was that love? She couldn't help wondering what she should do next. Oh, God, what was happening to her life? Was everything falling apart? She had to get things together. Had to know where she was going. Needed to know if this misery she felt was love, or just indecision. *Oh, God, I should know if it's love. Shouldn't I?*

CHAPTER NINE

Philippe drove slowly down St. Charles Street, absently weaving between the clanging streetcar and the traffic. He was oblivious to the sights and sounds around him, his thoughts centered on the spirited Cajun lady who had captured his heart, mind, and soul. In person, she made his past memories of her fade by comparison. He worried that he had loved a woman who didn't exist, that his need and desire for Noelle had made him embellish his memory of her, until he had created a creature far different from the real woman. Joyously, though, he found that she was everything he remembered, and more.

She was, in his imagination, everything his wife wasn't. *Warm, loving, supportive.* When he returned from Vietnam, he needed so much, yet all Marion gave him was a child. And that, begrudgingly.

Marion had wanted an abortion, for she knew the marriage was over. But he convinced her otherwise.

Philippe shuddered with the recollection. Thank God he had stood his ground. It had cost him enormously, but no value could be placed on his child. Then, to hurt him more, Marion had moved to Houston, making it difficult for him to be with his daughter.

Now all Philippe had was his fantasy-come-to-life, Noelle. He couldn't get her out of his mind. He wanted to be with her constantly, laughing and loving. He wanted to protect her, to help her out of this emotional stalemate she was in. Should he offer to get her a job at the company? No, she stubbornly wanted to do it herself. She had made that perfectly clear. At her present rate, she could damn well go down the tubes doing it herself! Oh, how he wanted to see her happy again, to wipe away her tears. To make love to her. Oh, God, he wanted her!

Philippe could feel himself growing tight inside with thoughts of Noelle enclosed in his arms. The mental image of her nude figure in the attic bedroom tied him in knots.

Philippe ran a cooling hand over his taut face, acknowledging that other, more serious thoughts occupied his mind this evening. He and Noelle had some deeper issues to discuss. Love, caring, and commitment—the future. He would reveal his feelings. He needed her and he could admit it—needed her in many ways. He needed to know how she felt about him, and in what direction she expected their relationship to go.

Was that too much to ask? He thought not. After

all, if he was perfectly willing to admit his love, why shouldn't Noelle? Philippe wanted a complete sharing of feelings tonight. With what he had to face, he needed her loving support. Now more than ever.

A frown creased his brow, and he reflected honestly. No, not more than ever. There had been a time when his life literally depended upon his mental and emotional attitude. His very existence was directly related to his will to live. The war's tragedies, his divorce, the deaths of his brother and father, all had taken a tremendous toll. Yet, somehow he had survived without Noelle.

The business had helped him keep going. It had to survive, and Philippe along with it. Betty Dunsmore had been an invaluable help there. She stood by him, and he managed to continue day after day.

He had dreamed of Noelle during that period. At times, they were beautiful, slow-motion images of the two of them walking or dancing or running hand-in-hand. That was when he was still in traction. Sometimes the fantasies of Noelle were erotic or full of fun and laughter. Her image danced before him or made mad, passionate love to him.

Those dreams were a part of the past. They had in some way sustained him. Now his life wasn't in danger. He would survive without her, although not happily. But that didn't affect his love for her, his desire to have her with him, always. Very soon he would tell her how much she meant to him.

He turned into the driveway of the old house on St. Charles Street and instinctively looked up to see the yellow glow from Noelle's bedroom window. Taking the stairs two at a time, Philippe's heart quickened at the thought of seeing her again. Of holding her again.

He knocked. The last time they were together was strained. Maybe it was the pressures of having Rose around. They had argued needlessly, and he regretted it. He had forced Noelle to listen to things she didn't want to hear. Of course, a person as intelligent as she could not hide from reality forever. Maybe he should let up on the sensitive issue. But, if he cared for her, he had to be honest, even if it hurt. If he really cared . . .

Noelle opened the door wrapped in her old garish, flowered robe. She smiled, faintly, not exactly sure how to greet him.

In Philippe's tiger eyes lingered a loving glow as he thrust a dress box into her hands. "Here's a little something for you, Noelle. I saw it and thought of you. Hope you like it."

She took the box and stepped back into the room. A gentle smile tempered her words. "Trying to make amends?"

"Yes." His honest brown eyes met hers levelly. "When we argue and are apart like that, I feel so empty without you. There are times when I think it's all my fault, others when . . ." He shrugged. "I don't know. Maybe you're right, Noelle. There are times when I don't understand you. But I'd like to try. Can we forget our misunderstandings for tonight?"

"I'd like that, Philippe. Come on in." She was taken by his honesty.

They sat opposite each other in the living room, eyes meeting, each drinking in the essence of the other. Her dark eyes were surrounded by faint bluish semi-circles. Noelle yearned to touch him, to feel his energy, to give him her love. Yet, she sat numbly, fingering the bow on the gift. He was so excitingly handsome, so strong, so masculine in his casual open-necked shirt and slacks. His face was honest, his expression revealing his desire.

"Well, open it," he encouraged her finally.

Noelle smiled and began to tear at the yellow ribbon encircling the box. In a moment she was digging into slick satin material. She held it up, then draped the emerald Oriental-style robe across her body sensuously. "It's . . . why, it's beautiful, Philippe. It's also very sexy!" She laughed aloud, knowing how utilitarian she must appear in her cotton chintz.

He folded his arms and assessed her with his head angled slightly. "I thought it looked like you, Noelle. The *real* you. Let's see if it fits."

Noelle rose and walked into her bedroom, overcome suddenly with a fit of modesty. Her fingers fumbled briefly with the top button on her robe. She felt him close, sensed his energy behind her. Then his exotic fragrance reached her and she breathed deeply, trying to preserve him forever in her senses.

Philippe's hands skillfully maneuvered over hers from the back, covering and caressing them. He pulled her to him, his chest against her back so that she could feel his breathing. She leaned her head against his shoulder and a sighing shudder rippled through her.

His voice was a low rasp. "Here, let me."

Her hands dropped limply to her sides, allowing him to completely unbutton the cotton robe. Gingerly his fingertips trailed sensuously from below her navel to the sensitive skin between her ribs and the heated valley between her exposed breasts. His hot palms centered over the firm tips of her breasts and he kneaded them passionately. While his hands caressed her nude body, his lips tormented her with feathery kisses across her neck.

Her body quivered irresistibly at his touch. "Philippe—" The sound came out as a gasp.

His hands continued upward to her shoulders, where he brushed the old robe from her, letting it drop to the floor. Noelle was nude and stood for an agonizing moment, her back to him. She reached, finally, for the new robe lying on the bed.

Philippe released his breath with a sigh and realized that he had been holding it in, all along. His tiger eyes glowed with passion at the ravishing sight of her slender form before him.

Noelle swished the silken emerald robe around her, then stepped away from him, modeling the new garment with an alluring smile. Her still-aroused nipples were outlined by the clinging material as it cascaded over her. She smiled up at him, her cheeks still flushed from the physical reaction to his touch.

"It's beautiful, Philippe. Thank you."

"Noelle, you're gorgeous. This color makes you even more desirable than ever." He reached forward instinctively and touched one breast, stroking her through the sensuous material.

She stepped to him, her arms wrapping around his neck. "Thank you, Philippe. I love it. When you touch me like that, I go crazy." With unfaltering eagerness she strained against him as her lips sought his. Her kiss was sweet and sensitive, giving him generously of her emotions. She opened willingly as his tempting tongue teased the edges of her lips. Within moments she was lost in the warmth of his embrace, the magic of his kiss.

Her silk-clad body pressed demandingly to his firmness, and Noelle became aware of what her feminine softness was doing to Philippe. It was an exciting, powerful feeling, and Noelle writhed erotically against him again. His hands circled her waist and pushed her gently away from him. He opened the front panels of her new robe, then allowed his eyes to drink her in hungrily.

"Ah, *ma petite,* the things you do to me. I like the way the robe fits you, but I like you even better without it." He rubbed her breasts with the backs of his hands as he slipped the robe from her shoulders.

Noelle caught her breath when the green satin fell away, and she stood exposed and vulnerable to his gaze. Philippe reached for her waist again and turned her around, then pulled her against him so she could feel his rigid manhood against her hips. It was a frustratingly sensuous feeling.

Meanwhile his hands created a wild rhapsody within her as they roamed from her taut, aching breasts, to her ribs, to her softly rounded belly, then to probe the silkiness between her legs. His hands cupped her femininity, pressing, piercing her soft warmth. She arched to meet his touch and a soft moan escaped her open lips.

"I want you, Noelle," he muffled against her hair, his lips seeking her earlobe.

"Yes, yes . . ." She moved stiffly toward the bed. By the time she removed the bedspread and turned back the blanket, Philippe was undressed and ready for her. He curled her back against his chest, and they lay like two spoons while his hands began an intimate exploration of her sensitive skin. One hand excited her velvety breasts and the other tantalized her madly, following every contour of her entire body.

As Noelle reached the peak of her endurance, she arched against his hands and begged for fulfillment. With masculine firmness Philippe pulled one of her knees close to her chest. His hands continued their provocative enticement while he thrust into her femininity.

Yielding to his direction, Noelle was propelled into ecstatic passion at the hands of the man she loved. Only Philippe could create within her such wild abandonment. With fervid zeal she moved to his rhythm, reaching exploding pinnacles in spasm after spasm. He held her tightly, his hands never loosening their grasp, wrapping her in the warmth of fulfilled love.

Finally, when both of them were spent and sated with the joys of what their love could bring, they curled in relaxed splendor. His lips pressed against her heated neck and his arms enfolded her securely. Noelle lay back against his chest, her arm flung around his neck, her fingers gently caressing his hair.

"Philippe . . ." she murmured softly.

"Hmmmm?" he muffled against her neck as his lips began to nibble at her shoulder.

"I have never felt so good. Never . . ."

"I can't believe we've missed this for so long. I've needed you, Noelle. Needed you desperately. I'm so glad you're here now. I need you more than ever . . ."

She closed his hand snugly over her tender breast. "Oh, Philippe, when I'm with you I'm so completely happy and I'm satisfied in ways that I never knew were possible."

"Making love to you is like nothing I've ever dreamed of. But there's more than that between us, Noelle—much more." He kissed behind her ear. *Why couldn't he just say he loved her?*

"Philippe, you're right. It's sharing and caring. In fact, I have something exciting to tell you tonight."

He sighed. Maybe she would make this easier, after all. "I have something to tell you, too, Noelle."

166

She shifted to face him and smiled happily. Her dark eyes glowed as she said, "I have a job offer!"

"Great, Noelle! Where? Doing what?" He shared her enthusiasm over the job offer at long last, but why did an ominous chill creep over him?

She touched his chest, relishing the feel of his curly hairs between her fingers. "This is exactly what I've been looking for—in teaching! However, it's both good and bad. Good, because it's teaching sixth grade." She paused, as if trying to anticipate his reactions to her next words. "Bad because the school is in Baton Rouge."

"Teaching? In Baton Rouge?" His words exploded angrily and he shifted up on his elbow so he could look at her closer. How could she even consider it? What was wrong with her?

Noelle spoke rapidly, trying to defuse his growing alarm. "Yes, teaching! Isn't it wonderful? The offer came through the State Board of Public Institutions and their statewide search. My only problem is the location. But I can manage that. *We* can manage that. Can't we?" She smiled imploringly.

Philippe shook his head slowly and looked at her with frustration. "Noelle, I thought we discussed this. You can't . . . just can't go back into teaching. And, in Baton Rouge, for God's sake!"

"What? And just why not?" Noelle demanded, sitting up with hands on her hips. Why couldn't he be as happy as she over her success? If he really cared, he would share her joy. He would understand.

"Because you're not ready, that's why! You need time. You aren't ready to go back into a classroom yet!" Philippe sat up and swung his legs off the side of the bed.

"If I have any more time without work, I'll be ready for the loony bin! Or the welfare line! I'm as ready for the classroom as I've ever been! Have you forgotten that teaching is what I do? It happens to be my career!" Noelle grabbed the discarded emerald robe and slid her arms into it.

"I really don't understand you, Noelle. I thought it was all settled." Philippe moved slowly to retrieve his slacks.

"You thought what was all settled?"

"That you wouldn't be teaching again. There are a million jobs you could do. Should do! It isn't fair to you or the students!"

"No, I didn't know it was all settled! To be quite honest, Philippe, I'm not convinced that I'm burned out. That's one of the little devices you dreamed up."

"Dreamed up! Noelle, that's crazy!"

She nodded emphatically. "And so are you if you think I'm not going after this job. I'm ready for it. Teaching is what I know best and what I do best! I'm going to Baton Rouge tomorrow!"

He jerked his shirt on. "You're the damned stubbornest female I've ever met! If you take that job, you're crazy. I'm definitely against it."

Noelle's eyes flashed angrily. "I don't remember

asking for your opinion or for your encouragement!"

"Good, because you'll get neither from me until you start being reasonable. Give me a call when you get your life in order, Noelle. I'll be interested to see what you decide to do because, believe it or not, I do care! Meantime, I won't be here when you get back from Baton Rouge. I'll be away . . . on business."

His words went unanswered, and she ignored the implications of his final remark. When the door slammed and he was gone, she felt a strange combination of relief and grief. She couldn't believe they had made wild, passionate love only minutes ago. How could she respond so deeply to a man who had no understanding of her feelings?

He didn't know, or care, about her true desires. There was only one kind of desire Philippe knew about. Sex! That's what their relationship was about, not love! Noelle had only dreamed of love. Well, it was over! She wouldn't succumb to her own weakness again! She was finished with Philippe.

She didn't need his constant discouragement toward her career. They were headed in different directions. Philippe was so fired up with his company, he couldn't understand her goals. Nor did he try. He was constantly working or going out of town on business. Even now, when she needed his support, he had more important business out of town. Well, so did she!

Noelle was so angry with Philippe and his blasted narrowminded opinions, she couldn't care less where he was going. Or why. She knew only that she was heading to Baton Rouge tomorrow, come hell or high water. She had a job interview, and it was about time!

The stifling fragrance hit her first. All schools must have the same aroma. Noelle would have recognized the school from the smell alone even if someone had brought her in blindfolded. Unconsciously, she wrinkled her nose.

She looked for the room with PRINCIPAL above the door and knocked on the frame, since the door was open. In fact, all the office doors were open. That was a good sign, Noelle decided quickly.

"You must be Ms. Clayton. I'm Betsy Wright, the principal." The woman extended her hand to Noelle and smiled pleasantly. "How was your drive from New Orleans?"

Noelle returned the smile and handshake. *So, B. Wright wasn't a man.* The principal was a very friendly, attractive woman with warm, understanding gray eyes. Obviously, an open-door policy was the way she worked. Things were looking better all the time.

"Nice to meet you, Ms. Wright. The drive was pleasant, thank you."

"Good," the older woman offered. "You probably want to stretch your legs. Why don't I give you a little tour of our school."

Ms. Wright was perceptive, too, Noelle concluded as she followed the principal from room to room.

She immediately liked this woman who might be her boss. Things were going well. Abruptly, Noelle was overwhelmed again by that pungent aroma. *Repulsive!* A bitter taste rose in her mouth and suddenly she felt hot. Tiny beads of perspiration broke out on her upper lip and between her breasts. She could feel it trickling down uncomfortably. *It's just chalk and books,* she told herself. All schools smell like this. But it was chokingly strong, and Noelle felt a bit shaky inside.

"Are you all right, Ms. Clayton? You look a little pale." The principal was very perceptive indeed. "Let's go to the teacher's lounge, and I'll get you a Coke."

Noelle accepted the icy drink and smiled wanly. What was wrong with her? She glanced about the pleasant yellow room and noticed, alarmingly, that the lounge had no windows. *No windows!* A lot of schools have inside rooms, she told herself. But suddenly the fact that the place had no windows took on monumental importance. She was surrounded! It had a smothering, closed-in effect.

"Feeling better now? Maybe you just need to walk. Let's see the art room. I know you're dying of curiosity. I think you'll like it." Ms. Wright's gray eyes smiled warmly at Noelle.

What is wrong with this woman? Can't she see that I feel worse, not better, Noelle thought in a panic. *I need to get out of this closed-in lounge.* A little fresh air sometimes works wonders. She gulped the Coke and followed the principal.

"This room doubles as a music and art room, with storage for each department at either end." Ms. Wright led Noelle into a long, somewhat narrow room.

There are no windows here either! And this is where I'd have to work!

Noelle's heart thumped rapidly as she walked numbly past the colorful storage lockers, stack of drums, shiny xylophones, and a spinet piano all the way to the far end of the room. There the walls were completely covered with poster-sized paper, decorated with childish patterns. Immediately those walls seemed to close in on Noelle, and she looked around frantically. How could she possibly work in this tiny, closed-in room? *Oh, I will manage,* she rationalized quickly. *I'll take my students outside to draw. But . . . not every day!*

The gaily colored paper danced wildly before her eyes. Noelle didn't know what was wrong with her. She had always loved children's artwork, but this time it seemed depressing, as depressing as the windowless walls. Ms. Wright chatted amiably as they continued to walk through other parts of the building, but Noelle was barely aware of what she was saying.

Noelle's mind whirled crazily and a certain thought began to form. It would not go away. *I can't do this . . .* It was as if her inner soul were working against her sense of reason. Was she losing control again . . . or gaining it at last?

"And this is the cafeteria. It doubles as a gymnasium."

Noelle's head snapped up at mention of the cafeteria, and she gazed apprehensively at the fold-up tables with benches attached and basketball hoops installed at either end of the room. *The cafeteria!* Noelle imagined spaghetti dangling from those hoops and green peas flying from table to table. And there she was, standing in the middle of the room screaming "Stop it!" utterly ignored by everyone.

She started to laugh at the image, a little hysterically, a little out of control. Quickly she snapped back to reality, forcing her emotions into a tight channel. Apologizing, Noelle mumbled something about how economical the design was, praying she had not said anything embarrassing aloud. Still, a tiny voice inside her mind was repeating *I can't do this! I've got to get out of here!*

Ms. Wright looked at her curiously, then suggested, "Shall we go back to the office?"

As the interview progressed, the conflicting thoughts within Noelle converged into one certain realization: *I can't do this!* She wanted to shout it out.

With considerable effort she managed to suppress the thought. Maybe it would go away. Maybe she could force it back. However, it continued to grow.

Finally there was a break in the one-sided conversation. "Well, Ms. Clayton, I see no problem with you starting to work here as soon as—"

"Ms. Wright, I'm sorry." The words rushed out

of Noelle's mouth before she knew it. And, once they started, she knew she mustn't stop. She had finally become aware of the truth about her situation. "I'm sorry, but I just . . . can't do this."

Ms. Wright shook her head. "I don't understand."

"I really don't understand either. It has nothing to do with this school, or you. It's *my* problem. You see, I've been teaching many years, and I love it. Love the kids. But I—I've been under considerable stress the past few months, and I . . . think . . . I think I'm suffering from burnout." There! She had said it! It was out in the open!

Ms. Wright looked at Noelle narrowly.

The admission, however, was liberating for Noelle, and she continued confidently. "Initially I believed this new teaching situation was right for me. That is, until I walked in here today. Now I realize it just wouldn't be fair to the kids, or to me. I'm sorry for taking up your time."

The principal's expression softened. "I'm sorry too. My impression is that you would make a very good teacher. But I understand what you're saying. I appreciate your concern for the children and wish you good luck." She stood to shake hands, mixed emotions obvious on her face.

Noelle fairly flew out of the building. She was free again! Free from the burden of guilt, free from the idea that teaching was the only fulfilling job for her. She felt light, buoyant, as she walked to her car. It was unbridling and wonderful and crazy! She threw her head back and laughed aloud.

Settling in the car, she grew somber. Noelle knew that the problem was still there in its disabling, embarrassing form. *Burnout.* But admitting it enabled her to begin to seek a solution. Philippe was right all along. Everything he said was true. The insomnia. The indecision. The dreading to go to work. The lack of control. Even the physical ailments. Philippe told her only because he cared. She could see that now. Oh, God, she couldn't wait to see him. To tell him! To hold him . . .

Oh, God, how she loved Philippe!

The two-hour trip from Baton Rouge to New Orleans seemed to last forever. She counted the minutes until she could rush home and call him. He would come over right away and . . .

Eagerly she covered the stairs two at a time and fumbled nervously with the key. Noelle rushed into the bedroom, grabbed the ivory and brass phone, and promptly dropped it. She scrambled on hands and knees for the receiver and with shaky fingers dialed his number. *I love you, Philippe! And you were right about my teaching; I need more time. Oh, Philippe, I know you care.*

The phone rang . . . and rang. No answer. Where was he? Vaguely her brain began to function. What had he said when they argued? She could only remember her part of that miserable conversation.

Her nasty comments, flung angrily at Philippe's puzzled face, came back to haunt her. He said he would be gone when she returned from Baton Rouge. *Gone!* But, where? *Away . . . on business.*

CHAPTER TEN

That weekend was the longest and loneliest Noelle had ever spent. Philippe was not at home, not at work, not available.

Noelle was beside herself with worry. Where could he possibly have gone? To Rosewood? But why? The place was hardly habitable. Besides, he admitted that he seldom went out there. It seemed an unlikely place for him to go. Business? On the weekend? Of course, that was a possibility. Sometimes he spent weekends in Houston combining business and time with Rose. But why didn't he tell her where he was going and when he would be back? Why didn't he call?

Why? She stopped short as the realization hit her. She hadn't even given him a chance to tell her where he was going. When they argued, Noelle had adamantly asserted that she was going to Baton Rouge with or without Philippe's approval. Her indication was that she didn't give a damn about his opinion! And, at the time, she didn't!

Another horrible thought struck her. Maybe he, like Noelle, had decided this was the end for them. What would she do without Philippe?

Noelle was so miserable with her imagination going wild that by Sunday she was frantic for something to do to take her mind off Philippe. In desperation she went to the one library that was open on Sundays and checked out a couple of books on burnout. She was a textbook case! It was a revelation to read some of her own symptoms! Philippe had been right. The signs of her problems were obvious to anyone who cared to look. She just hadn't cared to look. But Philippe had.

The book listed encouraging solutions. Noelle had to work on these. And she would too. She could work her way out of these problems, with Philippe's help.

Where was he? Noelle slammed the book shut and stalked about the room, hands jammed into her jeans pockets. Why hadn't she been more receptive to him? That's what he had talked about that night. But all she cared about at the time was her own selfish needs. Damn! How self-centered she had been! Oh, God, she missed him! She wanted to hold him and tell him . . . tell him how very much she loved him. Yes, love! *Love! I love you, Philippe Merritt!*

She lifted the phone again and rang his number. It was futile.

Sadly, she picked up the book again and thumbed through it, trying to concentrate on the solutions. *Separate work from private life; improve relaxation techniques; explore new options; develop a winning attitude.* She had heard these before, from Philippe. But at that time she had shrugged them off. She had scoffed at his textbook analysis of her problem. But here they were. Her textbook problems listed in black and white. Most importantly, there were reasonable, good solutions. Right now, for her, exploring new options seemed a good idea. Exploring new options . . . Noelle grabbed the Sunday morning want ads and began to search.

At 9:05 Monday morning, Noelle rang Philippe's office.

His secretary answered succinctly, "I'm sorry, he isn't here. May I take a message?"

"Betty, this is Noelle. Where can I reach him? I must talk to him!"

"Oh, hi, Noelle. How are you?" Betty's friendly voice delayed the answers Noelle wanted.

"I'm fine, Betty. I need to talk to Philippe. Where is he?" An unavoidable anxiety tinged her words.

After a slight hesitation, Betty replied. "Didn't he tell you? I . . . I'm not supposed to say, Noelle. He's in Houston, but can't be interrupted. I can give him a message for you."

"Houston?" Noelle's mind started whirling. "On business?"

"Uh, no, not really. I'll be talking to him later in the week and I'll—"

"No, Betty. Please, don't. He can reach me if he wants me." Noelle dropped the phone in its cradle with a clunk. Her heart dropped with it. *Houston!*

If not business, then why was he there? And why hadn't he told her? It must be personal, which would have to do with Rose. Was she ill? No, that wouldn't explain his instructions to his secretary not to reveal his whereabouts. He would want it concealed only if he had something to hide!

He was concerned about his relationship with his daughter and had said he wanted to spend more time with her. How would he do that? A shiver ran through her. How far would he go to improve the relationship with Rose? Marion was probably an attractive woman, and still unmarried. Noelle tried to shake off the thought that now haunted her. *Oh, God, no! Not now! He cares for me! I know it! He—he doesn't love her!* But, he had never said he loved Noelle. So, what made her so positive that he did? Just a feeling. And fervent hope.

Noelle sighed heavily, fighting back the tears that rushed to the surface. She grabbed the folded-up newspaper and began to study the red-circled items. She had plenty to do until she heard from Philippe. If she did . . .

Friday morning Noelle hovered over her cup of hot, rich coffee, staring red-eyed into its black depths. She should be happy, so why was she dragging around? She had a job. It was something new and different, so why wasn't she excited? She had come up with several good prospects. The new job might not be perfect, but it paid more than teaching. And it was definitely something she could separate from her private life. It was what she needed right now.

The ringing of the phone startled her. She looked at it expectantly, wondering if Philippe was on the other end. Well, there was only one way to find out.

"Hello?"

"Hello, Noelle?" With a pang of disappointment Noelle recognized Betty's voice. "Have you heard from Philippe?"

Noelle's heart thudded. "No."

Betty sighed loudly. "Well, I might get in trouble with the boss, but I think you could help, Noelle. I'll just deal with Philippe later."

"Help Philippe?" Noelle repeated curiously. What kind of help did he need? And from her?

"Yes," Betty continued. "I just talked to Philippe, and he sounded so depressed. If you would contact him, Noelle, I'm sure it would cheer him a lot. Maybe send him flowers or something."

"Flowers? Philippe depressed? What—what are you talking about?" Noelle's stomach lurched. *A wedding? Oh, no! He wouldn't go that far! Would he?*

"Noelle, I can't believe he didn't tell you about this. He—he really cares a lot for you, honey. But you know how men are. He didn't want anybody pitying him."

Noelle's head whirled. "Betty—what is it?"

"He's in Houston's Medical Center for some kind of repair surgery on his leg. This is about the seventh one he's had over the years, and he thought it would be old hat. But, of course, it isn't. He's in pain and all alone—"

Noelle was momentarily giddy, and she rambled incoherently. "Surgery? All alone? Surgery! Oh, thank God! I mean . . . oh, I mean poor Philippe, all alone! Is he all right?"

"Yes, the surgery went fine. But he needs you, Noelle."

Needs you. The words were music to Noelle's ears. "Oh, Betty, I can't tell you how much this means to me! Thank you, thank you! I'll certainly do everything I can to cheer him!" She was filled to overflowing with feelings of intense love and longing for Philippe.

"I'm sure you will," Betty answered, but Noelle had already hung up.

The short flight to Houston was too long for Noelle. She rushed through the airport, but took the time to make a local phone call, then hurried for a cab. "St. Luke's Hospital please. And hurry."

The driver nodded and took off with gusto. They began to weave in and out of Houston's wild traffic at a frightening pace. Noelle closed her eyes and said a quick prayer. Visions of her and this idiot cabby wrecked in a tumbled heap on a Houston street flashed through her mind. Oh, well, she and Philippe could share the same hospital room. She groaned at the thought and resisted the urge to tell the driver to make sure the ambulance took them to St. Luke's.

Miraculously, they arrived in one piece. She stopped by the information desk for Philippe's room number, then took the world's slowest elevator, becoming more and more furious as it stopped on every floor before arriving on his. Philippe's room was at the far end of the hall, and the walk took her forever. Noelle just couldn't move fast enough!

The sign on the door read DO NOT DISTURB. She knocked gently and pushed. She had been disturbed all week, and it was high time the disturbing was shared!

At the sight of Philippe, Noelle gasped. It was the first time she had ever seen him appear helpless. With one leg in traction, he didn't look like he could do a hell of a lot. That, alone, would be depressing to the man she knew. "Philippe?"

He turned his head toward her, and she could see from his expression what Betty could tell long-distance. He was definitely in pain. And miserable. Suddenly Noelle felt like crying and fought desperately to keep the tears down. This was not the time for tears. "Oh, Philippe. Why didn't you tell me?"

In an instant she was in his arms, pushing aside white sheets to press herself against his bare chest. The hot tears that she couldn't fight away fell on the curly hair as she buried her face and rained kisses over his chest, up his neck, finally reaching his lips.

Philippe's strong hand caressed her face and

wiped away the tears. "Hey, the wrong one is crying here," he teased, his voice rough with emotion. "I'm the one with the bum leg, see?"

She raised her tear-stained face. "I know. But it hurts me to see you like this, Philippe."

"Not as much as it hurts me," he chuckled.

"I wish you had told me about this surgery," Noelle admitted soberly. "I want to be by your side all the time. Especially when you need me."

"I can see that. And I'm sorry. I want you with me too." His hands cradled her face, and he kissed her lips tenderly.

"Actually, it's my fault. The night we argued, I didn't give you a chance to tell me anything," Noelle admitted. "I was selfishly thinking only of myself."

"There are so many things I didn't tell you that night, Noelle. Like, I love you."

She smiled confidently. "I know. I love you, too, Philippe."

His tiger eyes flickered warmly. "I'm not perfect, Noelle. Far from it. But, I do love you. Very much."

"You aren't perfect?" She smiled, taunting him with fingertips that drew sensuous circles on his bare chest. "You sure had me fooled. You make love perfectly. I can't imagine falling in love with anyone less than perfect!"

His hand slid along her back, pulling her against his sizzling skin. "I have a poor relationship with my daughter."

"We'll work on that," she promised.

"I'm cursed with a warped sense of what's good in music, according to a certain spicy Cajun lady I know."

Noelle wriggled lovingly against him and nodded in agreement. "You need some help in the music department, but when you hold me, Philippe, I'm in heaven. That's close enough to perfect for me."

"When I get out of here, I'll show you real perfection!" he threatened teasingly.

"I can hardly wait!"

"What about your perfect job, Noelle? Did you find it?"

She took a deep breath. "I finally realized that teaching in a school just wasn't for me, so I followed your advice and considered several other jobs. I thought about working in a record shop to sell my favorite Dixieland jazz music. Or I could open an art shop and sell the stacks of pastel drawings I made that week down on Jackson Square! I have enough to paper the walls with them! I could offer art lessons as well. But that takes money, which I don't have."

Philippe pursed his lips. "The art shop sounds like a good idea."

She grinned good-naturedly. "It is a good idea, but I have to continue to eat. And pay my rent. So, in the meantime, I interviewed for assistant art director at Louisiana Exports Limited."

"Limited!" Philippe exploded and attempted to rise. The tractioned leg swayed ominously, and he fell back on the pillow with a groan. "My God, woman! They're my biggest competitors!"

"Oh?" She ran a finger teasingly along his bottom lip. "Well, make me an offer."

"An offer? How about a proposal? If you'll marry me, Noelle, I'll dance at our wedding!"

"Dance?" Noelle looked at him in alarm. "Oh, Philippe, really? Do you think you should? You don't have to go that far!"

"Damn it woman! Why do you think I had this surgery anyway? I have to be able to dance with the two most important women in my life. You and my daughter." He motioned to the bandaged, tractioned leg. "They've added a piece of steel here and promised that I'll be able to do the Texas two-step! I'm now a man of steel, literally!"

"You were a man of steel before this surgery, Philippe Merritt!" she laughed sensuously. "I hope you didn't go through all this just so you could dance."

He smiled at Noelle's alarm. "Not exactly. But I instructed my doctor that as long as he was redoing this thing, to make sure I could dance a jig or two."

"Oh, Philippe . . ."

Her lips met his with a sweet, fervent force, binding them together in love . . . perfectly. Nothing could stop them now! "How soon can I get you out of here?" she asked in a low, sexy tone.

A firm knock at the door made Noelle jump up quickly. She blushed furiously, much to Philippe's delight, as the crisply white-garbed figure of a nurse entered the room. "Mr. Merritt?" the nurse said, "I have a visitor for you. She really isn't allowed in, but I told her she could just say hello for a minute."

Behind her, a beautiful blond child with brown, tiger eyes approached Philippe's bed. "Here, Daddy, I brought you something to make you feel better." A bouquet of a half dozen yellow roses were in her outstretched hand.

His muscular arms scooped up the child and her flowers. "Just having you here with me makes me feel better, Rosy."

She planted a kiss on his tan cheek and replied honestly, "Noelle said you just wanted to see my smile and that would make you feel better. But don't you like my flowers? I bought 'em specially for you!"

He laughed, and Noelle was relieved to see the taut lines around his eyes relax. "Of course I like them. They're beautiful. Just like you. Both of you. My two beautiful women."

He kissed his daughter's pert nose, then turned to Noelle. "Thank you," he mouthed silently over the child's blond head.

Though the nurse came to take Rose outside a few moments later, Noelle could see how much the short visit had pleased Philippe.

"Can I come see you again, Daddy?" Rose asked.

"Sure, sweetheart," Philippe mumbled as he pulled her close to him again for a goodbye hug, his eyes glowing.

After Rose had gone, Noelle sat down beside him.

She kissed his lips, then smiled happily. "I love you just as you are. Perfect!"

"You know, we've already reached perfection of sorts, Noelle," he commented wryly, then whispered in her ear, "in bed. But, of course, you know what they say about practice! When I get out of here—"

"What, Philippe? What will happen then?" Noelle said teasingly.

Philippe grinned devilishly at her. "When I get out of here, I'm going to dance with you. I want you to teach me to waltz, Noelle. Do you think I can learn?"

"Of course you can," Noelle said lovingly. "You can do anything. Anything you decide to do."

"With you by my side." Philippe looked seriously into Noelle's eyes. "Will you marry me, Noelle?"

"Yes, of course. I love you, Philippe. I have always loved you," Noelle murmured happily just before his lips closed securely over hers, turning their dream love into wonderful reality.

LOOK FOR NEXT MONTH'S
CANDLELIGHT ECSTASY ROMANCES®:

234 A BETTER FATE, *Prudence Martin*
235 BLUE RIDGE AUTUMN, *Natalie Stone*
236 BEGUILED BY A STRANGER, *Eleanor Woods*
237 LOVE, BID ME WELCOME, *JoAnna Brandon*
238 HEARTBEATS, *Jo Calloway*
239 OUT OF CONTROL, *Lori Copeland*
240 TAKING A CHANCE, *Anna Hudson*
241 HOURS TO CHERISH, *Heather Graham*

Candlelight
Ecstasy Romances™

☐ 210 **LOVERS' KNOT,** Hayton Monteith....................15080-9-77

☐ 211 **TENDER JOURNEY,** Margaret Dobson..............18556-4-19

☐ 212 **ALL OUR TOMORROWS,** Lori Herter...............10124-7-19

☐ 213 **LOVER IN DISGUISE,** Gwen Fairfax................15086-8-14

☐ 214 **TENDER DECEPTION,** Heather Graham 18591-2-16

☐ 215 **MIDNIGHT MAGIC,** Barbara Andrews..............15618-1-37

☐ 216 **WINDS OF HEAVEN,** Karen Whittenburg.........19578-0-29

☐ 217 **ALL OR NOTHING,** Lori Copeland 10120-4-13

☐ 218 **STORMY SURRENDER,** Jessica Massey 18340-5-10

☐ 219 **MOMENT TO MOMENT,** Bonnie Drake............15791-9-10

☐ 220 **A CLASSIC LOVE,** Jo Calloway.......................11242-7-22

☐ 221 **A NIGHT IN THE FOREST,** Alysse Rasmussen...16399-4-22

☐ 222 **SEDUCTIVE ILLUSION,** Joanne Bremer..........17722-7-28

☐ 223 **MORNING'S PROMISE,** Emily Elliott................15829-X-32

☐ 224 **PASSIONATE PURSUIT,** Eleanor Woods...........16843-0-16

☐ 225 **ONLY FOR LOVE,** Tira Lacy...............................16676-4-18

$1.95 each

At your local bookstore or use this handy coupon for ordering:

DELL BOOKS
P.O. BOX 1000. PINE BROOK. N.J. 07058-1000   B183A

Please send me the books I have checked above I am enclosing $ _____ (please add 75c per copy to cover postage and handling) Send check or money order – no cash or C.O.D.'s Please allow up to 8 weeks for shipment

Name _____

Address _____

City _____ State Zip _____